Magical Girl
Raising Project

MAGICAL GIRLS

SNOW WHITE

Can hear the thoughts of those in need.

RIPPLE

Can throw shuriken that always hit their target.

CALAMITY MARY

Can power up the weapons she wields.

RULER

Can order those directly in front of her to do anything.

TAMA

Can quickly open holes in anything.

NEMURIN

Can enter others' dreams.

TOP SPEED

Uses a broomstick to fly at high speed.

HARDGORE ALICE

Can quickly heal any wound.

Magical Girl Raising Project

1

Asari Endou

Illustration by Marui-no

YEN ON

NEW YORK

Magical Girl Raising Project, Vol. 1
Asari Endou

Translation by Alexander Keller-Nelson
Cover art by Marui-no

"MAHO SHOJYO IKUSEI KEIKAKU" by Asari Endou, Marui-no
Copyright © 2012 Asari Endou, Marui-no
All rights reserved.
Original Japanese edition published by Takarajimasha, Inc., Tokyo.

English translation rights arranged with Takarajimasha, Inc. through Tuttle-Mori Agency, Inc., Tokyo.

Yen On
1290 Avenue of the Americas
New York, NY 10104

Visit us at yenpress.com
facebook.com/yenpress
twitter.com/yenpress
yenpress.tumblr.com
instagram.com/yenpress

First Yen On Edition: June 2017

Yen On is an imprint of Yen Press, LLC.
The Yen On name and logo are trademarks of Yen Press, LLC.

The publisher is not responsible for websites
(or their content) that are not owned by the publisher.

Library of Congress Cataloging-in-Publication Data
Names: Endou, Asari, author. | Marui-no, illustrator. |
Keller-Nelson, Alexander, translator.
Title: Magical girl raising project / Asari Endou ; illustration by Marui-no ;
translation by Alexander Keller-Nelson.
Other titles: Mahō Shōjo Ikusei Keikaku. English
Description: First Yen On edition. | New York, NY : Yen On, 2017–
Identifiers: LCCN 2017013234 | ISBN 9780316558570 (volume 1 : paperback)
Subjects: | CYAC: Magic—Fiction. | Computer games—Fiction. |
Social media—Fiction. | Competition (Psychology)—Fiction.
Classification: LCC PZ7.1.E526 Mag 2017 | DDC [Fic]—dc23
LC record available at https://lccn.loc.gov/2017013234

ISBNs: 978-0-316-55857-0 (paperback)
978-0-316-56012-2 (ebook)

1 3 5 7 9 10 8 6 4 2

LSC-C

Printed in the United States of America

CONTENTS

Illustration by MARUI-NO
Design by AFTERGLOW

Go ahead!!

What Is *Magical Girl Raising Project?*

☆ Simple and fun for beginners, yet deep enough to keep experts addicted!
★ Beautiful card art from world-renowned artists!
☆ Highly animated characters like you'd find in an action game!
★ Five hundred character types and two thousand items! The combinations are infinite!
☆ Completely free to play! No purchase required—ever!

Welcome to a world of dreams and magic!

This is *Magical Girl Raising Project*, an RPG where you can become the ultimate magical girl! The Magical Kingdom has appointed you as Earth's guardian—a cute, fashionable, and powerful heroine, who must use her powers to fight against the forces of darkness! But don't forget the magical pals, costumes, magic items, and catchphrases you also have at your disposal. Defeat enemies to gain magical candies and become the magical girl of your dreams! The world is always in dire need of more of you, so be brave and take the first step! Your dreams will surely come true.

PROLOGUE

That night, Ako Hatoda was in a bind.

Having gone straight to her part-time job after school, it wasn't until she'd arrived at her front door, after walking home along the road with the lone bus stop, that she realized she'd lost her key. The small bit of metal would take forever to find under the best of circumstances, not to mention it was night out. It was fall, meaning the sun set earlier. Her only aids would be the weak light of the streetlamps and the moon.

Of course, she could just wait until her aunt and uncle came home to unlock the door. But that wouldn't change the fact that she'd lost the key... They'd have to change the locks in case someone picked it up and decided to use it. The last thing she wanted to be was an inconvenience.

Three months ago, her father had been arrested for stabbing her mother to death, and Ako's uncle, her mother's younger brother, took her in. She knew how much of a burden she was... She got to attend the same school, received an allowance, and wanted for nothing, but she was a constant nuisance.

She'd once visited her father in jail, but he'd turned her away, saying "Don't ever come back." At school, no one talked to Ako. For some reason, everyone knew about the argument between her parents that had turned deadly, and they whispered rumors about her incessantly. But no one talked to her. Ako was just a plague, a source of endless trouble for others.

So she decided to kill herself. Her mother had once complained tiredly, "You're as stubborn as your father," but the decision she'd reached seemed wholly reasonable to Ako. Better this than to remain a nuisance. She had slowly begun preparations for her suicide. She'd disposed of all her personal effects, had written her will, and had been steadily stealing her uncle's sleeping pills here and there so they wouldn't be missed, hiding them in her desk drawer. She only needed a little more to do the deed.

But now she'd gone and lost the key. The whole point of killing herself was to keep from causing trouble, yet here she was causing even more. Disgusted with herself for being stupid enough to lose her key at such a critical juncture, she sank down on the doorstep, hugging her knees. In her mind, the missing key became a symbol of everything bad in her life. It was all she could think about, and tears started pouring from her eyes.

"Are you okay?"

The voice was out of place. Maybe not so much around a middle schooler like Ako, but not one you were likely to hear in a residential neighborhood at night, and especially not one this adorable.

"If something's wrong, please tell me. Like...being locked out of the house because you lost your key?"

Ako looked up to see a girl so beautiful her heart raced just looking at her. Her white skin was almost translucent against the darkness of the night, her features all flawlessly arranged on her perfect face. Her smile was slightly awkward, and the contrast with her striking appearance made it that much lovelier.

Her outfit, however, was quite strange. At first glance, it seemed like a school uniform, but the style was way too garish. In fact, it was more like cosplay. She had a scarf fringed with frills and a skirt adorned with white flowers. Her armbands were emblazoned with some kind of school insignia, but it wasn't local. The same crest decorated her knee-high socks—no, they were actually white boots. The moonlight illuminated her platinum-blond hair, which was done up with a ribbon and flowers of purest white.

The words "magical girl" popped into Ako's head. Stunned, she somehow managed to convey that she had, in fact, lost her key. The girl nodded and said, "I'll be right back," then vanished with a gust of wind, a fruity scent tickling Ako's nose.

She had met a real magical girl.

Five minutes later, the girl returned, breathing heavily.

"Is this your key?"

It was indeed hers.

"Don't go losing it again, now."

The girl smiled, and Ako, captivated, stood to thank her. Somehow, even though they looked nothing alike, her expression reminded Ako of her mother, back when she still loved her father. It was a cheerful smile that made others happy to see it.

She bowed and thanked the girl, but when she looked up, no one was there. Her benefactor just had to have been a magical girl. Ako's spirits soared, and her heart felt warm. She didn't feel like dying anymore, now that she knew magical girls were real. She'd been saved. Ako wondered if she could become one, too—if she did, would people need her? The prospect was exciting. Did someone out there need Ako?

CHAPTER 1
BLACK & WHITE

After the government merged several municipalities four years ago, the harbor metropolis of N City became the largest city in the area. It encompassed the futuristic business sector, where uniquely designed buildings jutted up around city hall; mountainous villages, abandoned and left to rot; a great hospital, equipped with the latest medical technology; and a massive factory that had gone bankrupt and had to be demolished. Altogether, this formed a uniquely twisted city forced into being by the government.

And six months ago, reports of "magical girls" started flooding in from this N City.

As a car raced down the highway at blistering speeds well above the speed limit, the driver heard a knock on the window. He turned to look, thinking it was a rock, and discovered a smiling witch riding a broomstick. "You should slow down," she warned.

As a truck bore down on a child chasing a ball into the street, a girl clad in armor appeared between them and stopped the truck with her bare hands, then disappeared without a word.

As a guy hit on some young women and refused to take no for an answer, a girl with doglike ears ran up on all fours and dragged him away.

The only thing witnesses could agree on was that the girls were "too beautiful to be human." Yet their appearances, their clothes, and the situations in which they appeared were all scattered and unrelated. No one could tell the story the same way twice.

At first, people laughed it off as overactive imaginations, tall tales, and general BS. But the sightings continued pouring in, and a video of "Two Angels In Flight Holding Hands" was even uploaded to a video-sharing website, causing the rumors to spread like wildfire.

"It's real!" "No, it's gotta be a fake." In the workplace, in schools, on the Net—people everywhere were talking. Sometimes self-professed recipients of their help stepped forward and shared their stories, fanning the debate over the believability of the videos and the existence of these girls.

One witness swore that upon asking one, "Who are you?" the girl had answered, "I am a magical girl." It was at this point the "mystery girls" became "magical girls." Fan sites and research blogs cropped up one after another online, and aggregate sites updated daily with news about the sightings. One of the latest was particularly thrilling: A gunslinger girl like something straight out of a Western had raided the apartment of a triad gangster in the red-light district, beat up the bodyguards, and stolen all the money and guns inside.

"Hey, doesn't this sound like it actually happened?"

Three middle school girls sat waiting at a bus stop, one showing the other two the screen of her smartphone. On it was an aggregate site with the latest magical-girl reports.

"You really like that crap, don't you? No way it's real."

"What? It seems totally real, don't you think?"

"This article's *too* believable. It's like whoever wrote it was actually there."

"Yocchan, you always shut me down. Fine, so what if it does sound like they were there?"

"I shut you down because what you're saying is stupid, Sumi. If whoever posted it was actually involved, one of the gangsters or the mystery girl herself would have to have written an article, and they aren't gonna do that. Plus, aren't you too old for this?"

"Wouldn't it be cool if they did exist, though?"

The third girl, watching her friends' discussion, could no longer keep quiet.

"Yocchan, Sumi, you're both wrong. If magical girls were real, they wouldn't do stuff like that. They care about justice and helping people in need."

"Thanks for the flowery opinion."

"Yuki, your world is all, like, rainbows and unicorns, huh? It's almost delusional."

Behind the bus stop where the middle school girls argued over the rumors was a seven-story office building, the Seventh Sankou building. Atop its roof, a lone girl was considering the same article. She wore a Japanese kimono, but one showing enough skin to be a swimsuit. On her feet were extra-tall *geta* wooden slippers, a shuriken pin in her hair—all in all, more of a costume than an outfit. Only a magical girl would go out in public with such a getup in N City.

"Is this for real...?" she asked, pointing at the article on her magical phone. The heart-shaped screen shut off for a moment. Then, a light shone forth to form the holographic image of a sphere, hard and smooth like tile, floating in front of a lake background. Its right half was black, the left white, in an unsettling design. From its body sprouted one wing that fluttered like a butterfly's, scattering glittering scales into the air with every beat. Its face was an emoji-like smile, frozen in place and never changing, from which came a high, childlike voice.

This creature was Fav, a mascot character.

"It could be a fake, pon. Or it could be real, pon." The sphere did a flip and finished with a burst of sparkling scales. Blinded, the girl averted her eyes. "Calamity Mary could do something like this, pon. That silly girl loves to play the outlaw, so she tends to pull crazy stunts, pon."

Calamity Mary had laid claim to N City's Jounan district. Magical girls would often call the area under their protection their "land" or "home," but she more fittingly called it her "territory." Her actions warranted unkind descriptors such as "vulgar," "crude," "savage," and more. Even the mascot had belittled her with "outlaw."

"So it's true…?"

"Fav can't possibly tell you that, pon. If Fav spilled the beans every time someone asked what another magical girl was up to, Fav would be a tattletale, pon. And fairies hate tattletales, pon."

"Then what about this…?" She swiped a finger across the screen to a new page. Sightings of the "girl in white" vastly outnumbered those of all the other magical girls combined. She even had her own special section of the site dedicated to her. "I think that's too many sightings."

"Oh, Snow White's page? She works the hardest of all, pon. That's just the tip of the iceberg, pon. She works double, even triple what you see there for the good of the people, pon." The clearly inorganic black-and-white sphere with its organic-looking wing did two more flips and landed on a flower. "Ripple, weren't you looking at that site before, pon?"

"Was I…?"

"Is a rivalry brewing, pon?"

"No… I'm just surprised she works so hard."

"Rivalries are good in Fav's opinion, pon. It's a wonderful thing to have everyone competing, pon."

"Hmm…"

The girl, Ripple, looked away from her device, brought her dangling legs together, and dived from the edge of the roof she'd been sitting on, landing easily on the ground sixty feet below.

"Why'd you suddenly jump down, pon?"

"A pest is coming, so I just wanted to get out of the way…"

"A pest, pon?"

Ripple looked up from the valley between office buildings, and Fav followed her line of sight. A point in the sky grew steadily larger until it was recognizable as a person. Seeing who it was, Fav called out, "Top Speed!"

Top Speed, a witch riding a broom, descended into the concrete forest and peered at the other girl's face.

"How ya been, Ripple?" Ripple clicked her tongue loudly in response, and Top Speed smiled wanly. "Prickly as ever."

"I should have hidden faster..."

"We're both magical girls—we should get along more!"

"Shut up..."

"Well, anyway."

Ripple tsked in frustration again, but Top Speed paid her no heed. She was a stubborn sort—one of the reasons Ripple disliked her. That very stubbornness probably prevented Top Speed from noticing, too.

"Have you seen this article?" Top Speed held out her magical phone to show the news site she had been browsing. The gist of it was that the costumes of the rumored altruists in N City, aka "magical girls," resembled the ones in the popular mobile game *Magical Girl Raising Project*.

"A lot of people are connecting the dots. This could be bad, don't ya think?"

"It's not a problem at all, pon."

"Oh yeah?"

"If a magical girl was leaking information, that would be against the rules and a big problem indeed, but Fav knows none of you are so naughty, pon. News stories about us from regular people are just free advertisement, pon. It's wonderful, pon."

The little sphere had a tendency to talk like a salesman. When Ripple had first transformed, she'd pointed this out. Fav had unabashedly responded, "It's more like HR than sales."

About two months ago, Kano Sazanami had gained her costume and powers.

She'd heard the local legend that one in tens of thousands of *Magical Girl Raising Project* players had become real magical girls, but had never taken it seriously. From kindergarten through middle school, people had insulted her for no reason at all, and she'd always handled it by hurting them until they squealed and submitted. But when she started high school, various obstacles made it difficult to solve problems with violence.

The fifth would-be stepfather her mother brought home had touched her butt, a disgrace she had replied to with her fist before she packed her bags and left home. She found an empty apartment to live in by herself, and as long as she stayed there, she couldn't afford to get fired from her part-time job. As she fought through the mounting expenses, she also made sure to attend high school so she could have a future.

In order to keep herself employed and in school, she needed a hobby to relieve stress when things went sour. She also firmly believed that those who spent money on their hobbies were idiots, which made *Magical Girl Raising Project* a perfect match. So she added the game to her two other hobbies: reading manga in bookshops (without buying) and reading at libraries.

When one company succeeded in lowering prices on their smartphones, competing companies joined in on the price war. Three years ago, smartphones had expanded to 90 percent of the cell phone market, according to some reports. In the years to follow, demand continued to rise until they controlled the entire cell phone market.

And with the increase in smartphones came an upsurge in mobile games designed for them. Most of these followed the model of being free to download but requiring real money to progress smoothly. But *Magical Girl Raising Project* was completely free-to-play.

Kano had always scoffed at the immature boys at school talking about their games, but once she tried it herself, she was hooked. She'd designed her own avatar, the in-game representation of her player, then jumped right into the game. By clearing quests to help people and fight enemies, she could collect cards for

magic and items, strengthen her character, and take on more difficult quests and adversaries.

Sticking religiously to sessions of thirty minutes a day, she pro-
gressed at a snail's pace. But she still enjoyed gathering the cards
for her perfect strategies and combos, combining them, and win-
ning battles. With its perfect balance of hard work and reward, the
game brought her pleasure, and to a newbie like Kano, everything
was fresh and original. She didn't care much for magical girls,
but she remembered how, back when she still had a TV, she used
to smile along with the girls on-screen—and realized she had in
fact used to love them. Strangely, she found herself reveling in her
memories. Multiplayer battles and co-ops she found troublesome
and irritating, so she opted to play against the AI and clear quests
in the story mode. Progress was slow but steady. And a week after
she'd started the game, something changed.

Fav, the mascot character floating inside the screen, began
talking to her.

"Congratulations, pon! You've been selected to become a true
magical girl, pon!"

Thinking it was some kind of new event, Kano rapidly
skipped through the dialogue. Suddenly, the screen shone brightly,
and the blinding light enveloped her. The next moment, she had
transformed—she had become her game avatar, Ripple.

Kano took three deep breaths, looked at her hands and feet, then
checked her entire body in the mirror. Then repeated the process
four more times. She wasn't imagining things. She pinched her
cheek and felt the sharp pain—she wasn't dreaming. Searching for
a realistic explanation, she decided she must have been exhausted
from school and work.

"This is going to be a problem," she thought, and the next
time she looked in the mirror, she had detransformed. As a test,
she willed herself to change again, and she transformed in the
light. The same happened when she willed the costume away.
She repeated both processes over and over, and still she saw Ripple in the mirror. Her face, body—everything about her was

different from Kano, especially the salacious outfit she would never be caught dead wearing. The transformation was so real and vivid that she couldn't possibly consider it a dream or hallucination.

She flexed her right hand repeatedly, then drove her fist into her left hand. The sound wave and impact caused the windows to shudder and the ceiling light's pull cord to swing. Her fingers were like beautiful works of art—finer, longer, and more graceful than Kano's—yet held great strength within. She kicked at the floor lightly and almost hit her head on the ceiling. If she had cracked it, the landlord would yell at her again. Her physical power had increased by leaps and bounds, clearly no longer a normal human's.

Next, she examined her limbs and couldn't find any scars, bruises, or hairs—not even a mole or patch of dry skin. Her skin was smooth and soft, and firm as ripe fruit. Inside her body, energy coursed through her like never before. Outside, throwing knives and shuriken were sewn into her collar and sleeves. One unlucky slip and she could really hurt herself.

The rumors were true. The *Magical Girl Raising Project* game created magical girls.

She regarded the beautiful, perfect face in the mirror one more time. What was she, a model or an actress or something?

"Hmm…" Even her voice was different, higher and clearer than normal. She struck a few poses in the mirror—smiled brightly, blew a kiss. Everything she tried just looked right. Yet it was still a bit off from her idea of a true magical heroine. At the very least, it didn't feel orthodox.

"Something on your mind, pon?" the mascot asked from her phone's screen. Kano almost jumped, but somehow managed to keep her shock from showing. She couldn't do anything about the blush on her cheeks after getting caught striking poses and smiling in the mirror, though.

"Who are you…?" she asked, as calmly as possible.

"Fav is Fav, pon. If you played the game you should know who Fav is, pon."

"That's not what I mean… What is your goal?"

"Fav provides support to girls who show potential, pon. If you have any questions, don't hesitate to ask, pon."

He didn't seem to be listening. Ripple clicked her tongue and returned to the mirror. Staring back at her was, no matter how you sliced it, a magical girl. That fact was unmistakable.

"People described them as 'too beautiful to be human.' Is this really…"

"The ones you help will remember a little differently, pon. An average face will suddenly become 'too beautiful for this world,' pon. Is this unacceptable, pon?"

"No…"

Kano's avatar, Ripple, was based on a ninja—black hair, almond eyes, and thin eyebrows. She'd chosen her accessories in an attempt to compliment the half-kimono, half-swimsuit costume, yet seeing herself in full now, she looked rather plain for a magical girl. She sported a red scarf, the ninja cliché, and a giant shuriken hair clip that glinted silver. All else was a coordinated black, from head to toe. The name "Ripple" she'd come up with by translating her last name, Sazanami, into English, but in real life the Japanese outfit and Western name simply clashed.

"Is it possible to change your avatar's outfit?"

"Not at this stage, pon."

"Oh, I see…"

"What's the matter, pon? Something bothering you, pon?"

"No…"

Fav continued his explanation. Now that she had been chosen, she was expected to help people in need. Kano had no interest in helping others, but she couldn't resist the allure of beauty, superhuman strength, and the unrestricted use of magic.

More than anything, she was bored with her life.

"Fav will be sure to give you all the support you need, pon. For starters, take this magical phone, pon."

"What kind of support?"

"Fav is friends with every magical girl, so if you ever want to communicate, Fav can connect you, pon. Fav can also answer any of your questions, pon."

"What *is* a magical girl, anyway?"

"A magical girl is a magical girl, pon. Don't you watch TV, pon?"

"But what exactly does that mean?"

"The Magical Kingdom has granted you powers in order to help people, pon."

"For what reason? What is the Magical Kingdom's goal?"

"Don't you watch TV, pon?"

"Like I said…"

"You're a magical girl now, and that's final, pon. That is an irreversible truth, pon. No matter what you ask, no matter what the answer is, you are Ripple, pon."

"What?" It was all incredibly fishy, but she couldn't deny the extraordinary phenomenon she was now a part of. With enough effort, Kano could get into a good university, but effort alone couldn't make her into a magical girl. For that, she had needed a fair amount of luck and latent talent. If she let this chance pass her by, she'd most likely never get another one. So, after weighing her options, she made the calculated decision to accept.

Kano reflected on her objective pro-and-con calculations. As a self-professed realist, she was impressed at how calmly and collectedly she had accepted such an unusual situation.

Fav spoke up, possibly sensing her thoughts. "If you cannot accept that magical girls exist, you wouldn't have been chosen as one in the first place, pon."

She wasn't allowed free rein right off the bat, though. When Fav informed her she would need lessons from a more experienced mentor, Kano became moody. Just imagining it rubbed her the wrong way.

"Fav, you said you would be my support…"

"Fav would love to help as much as possible, but there is only one of Fav, pon. Fav cannot do everything, pon."

Kano remembered the game's forced tutorials and how slow and frustrating they were—simple button-clicking over and over, clearly made for idiots with no imagination. She shut off her new magical phone and clicked her tongue angrily. She could barely stand to look at the heart-shaped screen.

Talking to others had never been Kano's strong suit. To be honest, others in general had never been her strong suit. She had a deep dislike for people who herded together and thought they were tougher for it. This was one of the reasons she'd started playing *Magical Girl Raising Project* in the first place, so the looming prospect of obnoxious human relationships upset her.

Her first impression of Top Speed, her mentor, was that she seemed like an idiot. She wore a triangular witch's hat and a witchy dress and carried a magic broom. She was your generic spellcaster, and even her face appeared more Western than Ripple's. Her big blue eyes, a classic magical-girl trait, darted about busily as she tossed her flaxen braids. Only her long purple cape and the charm hanging from her neck broke the witch archetype in any way. The back of the cape, Ripple noticed, was embroidered with the words "No Gratuitous Opinions."

Oh, she's an idiot, Kano thought to herself, and her appraisal dropped even more. They'd agreed to meet on the roof of the Seventh Sankou building, and as Top Speed landed she gave a big smile and jabbed her right hand out in a thumbs-up.

"Nice to meet ya! I'm Top Speed. Good to have ya on board!"

"...Nice to meet you."

"Where's your energy, man? You eating right? Ha-ha-ha!"

She spoke like a guy and cackled like a fool. Ripple's assessment slipped down another level.

With a flourish, Top Speed spun and parked herself on the guardrail and beckoned Ripple to sit beside her. Not wanting to sit next to her, yet also not wanting to stand under her gaze, the ninja chose the simplest option and leaned against the wall.

Top Speed then proceeded to explain all that being a magical girl entailed. In essence, they used magic to help normal people, and doing good deeds earned them magical candies.

"Good deeds...?"

"In the game, you'd defeat enemies and stuff, but in the real world there ain't much in the way of enemies to defeat, ya know? I know it's not glamorous, but honest work like this is best." Top

Speed spoke with an air of experience, but Ripple just scoffed silently.

Top Speed also taught her functions of the magical phone that only they could use—although it was nearly identical to a regular smartphone. The way Top Speed talked it up only added to Ripple's exasperation. She did not show this, of course, but silently scoffed again.

Following instructions, Ripple used the device to bring up a page with her personal data. Height, weight, and measurements—it was all there. As Kano, she was an inch taller than the average boy and solidly built, but when she transformed into Ripple, everything about her became feminine. Under "Personality" was written "Violent and unsociable," and the fact that she agreed with this just irritated her more. Under "Magic" was written "Throws shuriken that always hit their target," and this time she audibly clicked her tongue.

"Hmm? What's up?"

"I only have one kind of magic..."

It was so plain. Throwing shuriken was more of a ninja technique than a power. She could think of so many other ninja-like things to do, like creating clone illusions or breathing fireballs.

"Magical girls only get one kind of magic, see. It was way easier in the game when you could use lotsa magic, but them's the breaks."

That wasn't the only depressing piece of information Top Speed had to share, though. There were also two rules that all magical girls had to follow: Never reveal yourself to a regular human, and never talk about the rules or your powers to a regular human. Those who broke these rules had their right to be magical girls rescinded.

Once a week, they had an online meeting. While attendance was not mandatory, it was a good idea to attend so as not to miss some major announcement.

Certain members of their ranks were very territorial. The two places to avoid in the city were Calamity Mary's Jounan district and

Ruler's Nishimonzen. The former loved to pick fights, and the latter was just aggravating to listen to. Both were an equal pain in the butt.

Top Speed regaled Ripple with stories. For instance, Sister Nana had once stumbled into Calamity Mary's territory and was nearly killed for it. There was also the time a video of the Peaky Angels had made its way to the Internet and caused a stir. The more she talked, the more Ripple checked out. When her mentor had finally finished, hopped onto her broom, and disappeared into the night sky, Ripple clicked her tongue.

"Hey…"

"Yes, pon?"

"Who made her a mentor?"

"Friendly magical girls volunteer for the job, pon. Top Speed's explanation might have taken three times longer than normal, but that just shows how thorough she was being, pon."

So not only had she been the victim of an overzealous busybody, but she had also suffered through a longer-than-necessary introduction. Ripple clicked her tongue louder than she had in years. To her, Top Speed had gone from "idiotic mentor" to "idiot trying to act like a mentor."

For some reason, Top Speed kept coming back to visit Ripple. Not even subtle sounds of dismay or saying to her face, "You don't have to come back" could stop her. She simply waved it away with a, "You're such a prickly pear."

Realizing words wouldn't reach her, Ripple decided to ignore Top Speed. In the end, the witch would talk without interruption until she'd had her fill, then leave for the day. One time she brought a plastic container of boiled sweet potatoes, which Ripple grudgingly tried and found delicious.

◇◇◇

In summer, Kubegahama practically teemed with tourists, but by fall it was a ghost town. When the sun set, not a soul could be found wandering the streets. A very tall steel tower stood on a hill overlooking the beach, and on this tower sat two girls in costume. One of them wore a white school-uniform-esque outfit, and the other looked at first glance like a knight from the Middle Ages, but with a long tail. The two of them huddled close around a magical phone and spoke with the mascot character, Fav.

Magical girls preferred constructs like office buildings and steel towers. These tall, deserted areas were good resting spots where their outrageous outfits could go unnoticed. Few of them could truly fly, but they all had the ability to run up building walls as if they were flat ground.

"Be extra sure to come to the next chat meeting, pon."

"Why?"

"There's going to be an important announcement, pon."

"I heard a new girl was joining. Is it that?"

"That, and a big event as a result, pon."

"What kind of event?"

"You'll have to show up to find out, pon."

"Hmm."

Snow White turned off her phone and rotated a little to the side. She drew her knees close to La Pucelle's, making it easier to converse.

"Sou, Sou. Did you hear that?" she chirped.

"I did."

In contrast with Snow White's ill-fitting nonchalance, La Pucelle's response had a tinge of melancholy to it.

"What do you think?"

"Chat attendance has been low lately, so maybe Fav is doing this to get people to show up."

"It's low?"

"Yes. Yesterday only seven people showed up: you, me, Nemurin, Cranberry, Top Speed, Sister Nana, and Winterprison."

"But that's higher than before."

"It's still low. Can you recall even one time when everyone showed up?"

Attendance at the once-a-week chat meeting was recommended

but not mandatory, which was causing a drop in attendees, a situation Fav was always trying to remedy. He constantly insisted that everyone should exchange information more, and that they should be friendlier toward one another. Hardly anyone listened.

Snow White and La Pucelle both had a high attendance rate. They were huge fans of magical girls and jumped on every chance to associate with others like them. Thanks to the chat meetings, they had developed many friendships, so to them, at least, the meetings had not been for nothing.

"That chat room is so tiny. I think it'd be really hard to squeeze lots of people in."

The weekly chat took place in an imaginary meeting room, with each girl entering as a simplified version of her avatar.

"It's not like we'll be literally squeezed, so what's the problem?"

"Still, Sou…"

"Also!"

La Pucelle jabbed her pointer finger at Snow White, who stared blankly back.

"Don't call me Sou when I'm transformed!"

"Oh! Sorry, So—" Snow White started to apologize but made the same mistake again, so she laughed to try to cover it up. Her infectious laugh caused La Pucelle, finger still extended, to start giggling as well.

Koyuki Himekawa had always admired magical girls. As a child, watching the adorable Hiyoko in the *Hiyoko* series had been an emotional roller coaster. From there, she had moved on to the *Star Queen* series and the *Cutie Healer* series. Watching these brave girls fight against evil enthralled her. Her childhood friend and fellow magic fan would also borrow older series from a cousin for them to watch, which introduced her to girls like Merry, Riccabel, and Miko. They used their powers to bring people happiness and never faltered, no matter what the danger. Koyuki even declared that when she grew up, she'd become a magical girl just like them, which made her friend jealous, since he could only hope to become a sorcerer.

As the years went on, more and more of her classmates began to consider magical girls childish, but even in high school Koyuki stubbornly stuck to her beliefs. To her, they weren't just fiction—they had become an irreplaceable part of her being. But she knew people would only mock her wish to become one and help people if she ever voiced it, and so she kept it to herself. But she just couldn't bring herself to abandon her dream.

It was in middle school that Koyuki first came across *Magical Girl Raising Project*. It was inevitable that a girl who'd wished all her life to become a magical do-gooder would learn of a game rumored to grant that wish. Still, she didn't start the game convinced it would actually happen. Her reasoning was something like, "*It's just a rumor that people actually transform, right? Yeah, they're just rumors. But it's okay to just wish that they're true, right? I still like magical girl–themed games, anyway. Besides, it's free!*" Twenty-eight days after starting the game, Koyuki Himekawa became Snow White.

When she looked in the mirror, she could see the figure she'd dreamed of since she was a child. She hadn't just dreamed, but had drawn it out on paper. She'd based the outfit on the school uniform from the most popular manga at the time and, as the name "Snow White" indicated, made her outfit entirely white and decorated it with white flowers. While Koyuki had rarely been called lovely, let alone beautiful, the girl in the mirror was truly beautiful. Her skin was a translucent white, her eyelashes long. Snow White was an entirely different person from Koyuki, but it didn't seem odd that they were one and the same.

She didn't think she was dreaming, either. The experience was surreal, for sure, but also overwhelmingly authentic. She jumped and squealed with joy, smacking her head on the ceiling and then falling on her butt. Her mother, surprised by the noise, came to her room to investigate. Fortunately, Koyuki managed to change back in the nick of time and convince her mother she had simply tripped. As a normal human once more, she started to think that maybe it all had been a dream, but then she transformed again.

And there stood the magical girl Snow White.

"Yes… Yes… Yesss!"

"Congratulations, pon."

"Yes! Yes! Yesss! Thank you, Fav! I'm so excited to start!"

She spent the rest of that day smiling so widely her mother began to worry she'd hit her head. That night she snuck out to school, careful not to get caught by her parents. Late at night in the empty school yard, she hopped, leaped, kicked, punched, flipped, and somersaulted, slowly unleashing more and more of the power welling within her, discovering new moves she could never have done before. She had really become the heroine from her imagination. When the realization finally hit her, joy and excitement overwhelmed her without giving her a moment to breathe.

She did a somersault again, and her skirt flipped up. Perhaps she should have made it a little longer—compared to her school uniform, it was extremely short. She made a mental note to keep her actions more restrained in front of others.

"Oh, can I use any magic?"

"You should check the personal data on your magical phone for that, pon."

She turned on her new gadget and consulted the page listing various details on Snow White.

"Hey, Fav."

"Yes, pon?"

"Under personality it says 'clumsy' and 'strong sense of justice,' which is fine, but what's this 'tendency to daydream'?"

"Humans find it difficult to view themselves objectively, pon."

"Really…?"

Under "Magic" was written, "Can hear the thoughts of those in need," the perfect ability for Koyuki's ideal, the champion of the people. She was so grateful to the ones who made this possible. *Thank you, Magical Kingdom. Thank you for giving me this wonderful power.*

That day marked Snow White's debut. Every night she'd sneak out her window to look for people to help: a middle schooler who'd lost her house key, a university student who'd had their car stolen, and a businessman under pressure for money, to name a few. There were also many troubles she couldn't do anything about, like concealing adultery, a boy unsure of whether or not to confess to the girl he had a crush on, or a retiree desperate for their pension.

Hearing the thoughts of those in need was the only special ability she possessed, so the only way she could help was to roll up her sleeves and join the fray with her magically enhanced arms, legs, eyes, and ears. However, the problems that could be solved this way were endless, and so work was never in short supply. Only two days after her first transformation, she was earning magical candies left and right, and the candy warehouse in her phone was filled with bottles—and she hadn't even met her mentor yet.

At her first chat session, the girls welcomed her with open arms. There was Top Speed, her avatar dressed like a witch; Sister Nana, clad like a nun; Weiss Winterprison, dressed in a long scarf; Nemurin, wearing pajamas; Musician of the Forest, Cranberry, draped in flowers; and La Pucelle in knight's armor. Top Speed shared her experiences, cracking jokes the whole time, while every now and again Sister Nana would interject with her own. Nemurin hardly spoke, saying she preferred to listen to what others had done. The silent Winterprison simply stood at Sister Nana's side as Cranberry played music from her chair in the corner.

Just as the meeting was about to adjourn, La Pucelle approached Snow White. As it turned out, she was in charge of the area just next to Snow White's and had volunteered to be her mentor. They agreed to meet at midnight the next day at the tallest steel tower by the Kubegahama beach.

Koyuki had never met another magical girl in real life before, and the excitement caused her to space out even more during class. She received three warnings from her teacher that day, and even her friends worried something was wrong. Becoming a magical girl hadn't changed Koyuki's passion for them in the slightest, and now she was going to meet and talk to one face-to-face. And not as a fan and celebrity, but as fellow heroes. It was impossible to calm her racing heart.

That night, she made sure not to be late by arriving fifteen minutes early, but when she climbed the steel tower she found La Pucelle already there. Magical girls possessed great night vision, so even on that moonless night, she could see clear as day the lone knight standing at the top of the tower. Her armor consisted of wrist guards, a breast guard, and shin guards, with a giant sword more than a foot wide and a yard long slung across her back. An image of a fiercely roaring dragon decorated the sheath. Hornlike hair decorations and a tail accessory extending from her waist completed the dragon imagery.

Her magical girliness—her femininity—however, was still quite apparent even under all that armor. Where some might cover up, she left her cleavage and thighs clearly visible. Her hair was done up just so, barely touching her shoulders, with a few strands dangling from each side of her head. La Pucelle heard Snow White arrive and shifted her gaze from the ocean to Snow White. Her expression was regal, but she also seemed uncomfortable. Snow White panicked, thinking she'd shown up late.

"U-um, it's nice to meet you… Well, we've talked before, via chat, so it's nice to meet you in person? Is that okay? Anyway, it's nice to meet you!"

It wasn't a very good greeting. In fact, it was fair to call it terrible. And Snow White, head bowed deeply, knew that more than anyone.

She glanced at La Pucelle. Arms crossed, the other girl gave three deep nods. "I knew it," she said with a husky voice. "Koyuki?"

Question marks flickered in Snow White's mind at hearing her name from this person she'd never met.

"H-how do you know my real name?"

"I knew it was you. It's me, Souta."

"Huh?"

"Souta Kishibe. We went to the same school until two years ago. Don't tell me you've forgotten me."

"Wh-wh-whaaaaaaaaat?!"

The reason Souta Kishibe had realized Snow White's true identity was simple—she closely resembled the drawing of a magical girl Koyuki had labeled her "grown-up self." Souta, her childhood friend, had seen her draw it—even memorized it. The first time he saw Snow White's avatar, he had suspected it might be her. Meeting her in person just confirmed it.

The reason Koyuki Himekawa hadn't realized La Pucelle's real identity was equally simple. She never could have imagined that tan, energetic, soccer-loving boy as a regal female knight. Even knowing the transformation could change one's body, clothes, age, and physical prowess, she had never guessed it could also change one's gender. The two of them sat next to each other on the steel tower and chatted until the sun was nearly risen, rekindling their old friendship.

"So was it *Magical Girl Raising Project* for you, too, Koyuki?"

"Yeah. One day Fav just started talking to me. I thought it was some sort of event, and the next thing I knew I was a magical girl. How long have you had powers, Sou?"

"About a month, I think. Man, I'm so surprised you ended up one."

"Hey, I've always loved them! I'm more surprised at you."

"I've always loved them, too, you know. I just didn't tell anyone," Souta said. There was a world of difference between boys and girls liking this sort of thing. In middle school, a girl would be considered odd, while a boy would be considered a pervert. He'd had to walk a town over to get his fix at the DVD rental shop where no one knew him and conceal his manga and light novels inside his school desk, hiding like a Christian in the Edo period.

"Sou, I thought you forgot all about magical girls and went for soccer instead."

They'd been forced to go to different middle schools because they lived in different districts, but Koyuki had seen Souta running during early-morning practice many times.

"Soccer's fun, but it can't scratch the same itch."

"I wonder if there are any other boy magical girls."

"According to Fav, I'm the only one in the area, and even globally it's pretty rare."

"Are you really a girl now?"

"When I transform, I'm completely female. Yeah, no doubt about that."

For some reason, La Pucelle's cheeks reddened slightly with embarrassment.

They made two rules: to work together, and to always stay in character, even when they were alone. And so the Snow White–La Pucelle duo was formed. Voices from those in trouble reached Snow White's ears, no matter how big or small the problem. Using her magic, she roamed the city searching for people to help. La Pucelle became her partner, but her magic was not as peaceful as Snow White's. It was much more violent. La Pucelle appointed herself the role of bodyguard, insisting she would protect Snow White if something ever happened. Not that anything could threaten a magical girl.

CHAT #1

The goal of *Magical Girl Raising Project*'s chat function was to allow the players to communicate through their avatars. Thus, the weekly chats also made use of this function. The chat room, modeled after a conference room, opened its doors, and one after another, the little characters made their way inside.

☆ Cranberry has entered the Magical Kingdom.
☆ Magicaloid 44 has entered the Magical Kingdom.
☆ Swim Swim has entered the Magical Kingdom.
☆ Top Speed has entered the Magical Kingdom.

Magicaloid 44: Greetings
Top Speed: Sup
Cranberry: ♪

☆ Snow White has entered the Magical Kingdom.
☆ Tama has entered the Magical Kingdom.
☆ Nemurin has entered the Magical Kingdom.

Snow White: Good evening! Nice to see you all!
Swim Swim: Yo
Tama: Arf!

☆ Ripple has entered the Magical Kingdom.

Top Speed: Wow, look who finally decided to show!

☆ La Pucelle has entered the Magical Kingdom.

Nemurin: Hi
Magicaloid 44: Greetings, rare character

☆ Ruler has entered the Magical Kingdom.

La Pucelle: Good evening, ladies

☆ Calamity Mary has entered the Magical Kingdom.

Ruler: Evening.

☆ Sister Nana has entered the Magical Kingdom.
☆ Winterprison has entered the Magical Kingdom.

Sister Nana: Good evening, everyone. Blessings to you all.
Winterprison: Hey

☆ Minael has entered the Magical Kingdom.
☆ Yunael has entered the Magical Kingdom.

Calamity Mary: *This message cannot be displayed due to bad language.*
Yunael: Hiya!
Minael: Yay!

☆ Fav has entered the Magical Kingdom.

The chat room was crammed with avatars.

Musician of the Forest, Cranberry flopped back onto the bed she'd been sitting on, magical phone in hand, and rolled over the old sheets onto her stomach. Her hair, fixed with a flower-shaped clip, flipped up softly and brushed against her waist.

If the top of a tall building was the perfect resting spot for magical girls, then an abandoned cabin in the middle of the mountains was the perfect residence for them. Someone like Cranberry, who had no life in the human world, needed only solitude and a roof over her head. The resort hotel near the peak of Mount Takanami, abandoned halfway through construction, had fit her needs for over half a year. No one knew she was there.

Thanks to Fav's insistence that there would be an important announcement, no one had attempted to skip out on that week's chat. Some, like Ripple, were clearly there against their will and remained sullenly silent without even an attempt at a greeting, but still, every magical girl active in N City was accounted for. This had never happened once since the weekly chats had begun, and the small room was packed like a can of sardines.

> **Top Speed:** Hey, weren't we getting a new girl?
> **Fav:** Oh, that's next week, pon
> **Fav:** Although, this conversation does involve her...

In total, there were fifteen magical girls active in N City, which meant adding a new one the following week would bring the total to sixteen. That was too much, even for a metropolis like N City. The mana that powered their magic depended on the land and was, consequently, a limited resource. The addition of another would drain mana from the land even faster and deplete it in no time.

After summing up the current situation, Fav eagerly made his big announcement.

> **Fav:** And so, we'll be cutting down on the number of magical girls, pon. Half—eight—is our goal, pon

The room was silent as the girls processed what Fav had just said. A moment later, a storm of criticism, a tide of complaints, and an endless stream of questions and concerns followed. The size of a rock is most understandable from the splash it makes. Speech bubbles from the avatars covered the screen, filled with everything from all caps to colored text, and it became nearly impossible to see anything in the already tiny chat room. Fav bowed and apologized over and over. He even seemed to be shedding fewer scales than normal.

Exactly what method would they use to cut down the numbers?

Fav: This magical girl chat is held once every week, pon
Fav: so once a week we will announce who has been cut here
Fav: for eight weeks until eight of you have been let go, pon
Fav: The one with the fewest magical candies
Fav: will be the one to go, pon

Cranberry was well aware that nobody was about to say, "Who do you think you are, pretending like nothing's wrong when we're in this thanks to your incompetence? If that's how it is, I quit!" They had all joyously accepted their new status as magical girls. Tasting such great power and then losing it would upset anyone. The higher they rose, the harder they fell, and the deeper they despaired.

Fav: To repeat:
Fav: Once a week, the girl with the fewest magical candies will be cut, pon
Fav: So please work your hardest to gather lots of candies, pon
Fav: Fav is very, very sorry for the inconvenience, pon
Fav: Oh, and
Fav: there has been an update to your phones, so please be sure to check that out, pon
Fav: That's all, pon
Fav: See you here in one week

Cranberry logged out from the chat, turned off her device, and threw it at her pillow.

◇◇◇

In the week after the chat, magical-girl sightings spread like wild-fire. The Internet was blowing up.

A princess chased away a scary dog.

Twin angels flew through the sky to recover a lost balloon.

A girl in a white school uniform helped push a car out of a ditch.

The farther they spread their activities, the more chances there were for them to be seen. They were desperate to gather as much magical candy as possible to increase their chances of ending up in the final eight, which drove up reckless exposure, traffic for news sites, and public awareness.

"Whatcha lookin' at, Ripple?"

Ripple, sitting on the roof of an office building, heard a voice from above. She continued to stare at her magical phone, neither answering nor turning toward the sound.

"Oh, is that the news? Everyone's working so hard now, huh?"

Top Speed alighted next to her, and Ripple finally turned her head.

"Snow White's really working her butt off. Geez, save some for the rest of us, right?"

Sightings of the white magical girl were leaps and bounds ahead of sightings of the others. She wasn't even doing anything spectacular. Her assistance came in small, everyday actions like picking up dropped change, ferrying forgotten lunches, and reminding people to zip up their flies. Was helping with mundane difficulties a magical girl's true purpose? Or was she simply not capable of undertaking greater issues? According to the Internet, at least, it appeared to be the former.

Snow White was the pure and righteous heroine little girls dreamed of becoming—the exact opposite of Ripple, who brushed off praise for her work by saying she was simply "in it for the candy." It wasn't that Ripple didn't want to serve the community, but she was too embarrassed to say otherwise. However, maybe boldly declaring, "I want to help others!" and actually doing so was the correct way to be a magical girl, she mused.

"Ripple, you're really focused on Snow White, ain't ya? She your rival?"

Ripple clicked her tongue sharply. The voice felt like cold water jolting her out of her reverie.

"I thought you considered Calamity Mary your rival."

Another disapproving click. *And who exactly was responsible for that mess in the first place?*

A few days after Ripple had first transformed, Calamity Mary had come knocking on the roof of the Seventh Sankou building, Ripple's and Top Speed's de facto meeting point. Light as a butterfly, she had leaped to them from a neighboring building. As she landed on the roof, Ripple noticed she looked exactly as the rumors stated: like a cowgirl. *Not really magical girl–esque*, she thought, though she didn't have any room to judge.

Calamity Mary's business with them was quite simple.

"You, little girl. Ripple, was it?"

She appeared to be in her second or third year of high school, and she was much more well-endowed than either Ripple or Top Speed. Her breasts and butt were huge. Ripple looked like she was in middle school, which made the "little girl" comment somewhat understandable, she reasoned. So, while it did irk her a bit, she kept her cool and give a small nod.

Calamity Mary flicked her cowboy hat.

"I told Fav I'd be mentoring the next newbie."

"Oh, y'see, I made Fav promise me a long time ago that if a new girl was assigned to a neighborhood near me, I'd get to mentor her. Good neighbors and all that, right?"

Ripple had been assigned to Nakayado, the center of an area once famous as a castle town, while Top Speed's area was the northern section of Kitayado. Naturally, they were next to each other.

"It was a really long time ago, so that must be why Fav came to me first. I had no idea you two had an agreement. I'm so, so sorry."

"Oh?"

Calamity Mary continued to stare at Ripple, sparing no concern for Top Speed groveling with her hat in her hands. Ripple glared back. The uncivilized staring was upsetting enough without Top Speed kowtowing to someone who was ignoring her entirely.

In a flash, Calamity Mary's gun left its holster and fired at Ripple, who whipped out the sword from the sheath on her back and deflected the incoming bullet. Not a tenth of a second had passed before it was over. Flustered, Top Speed raised her head.

"What're you two doing?"

"Ain't it obvious? Huh, little lady?"

Ripple glared hard at the pistol in Calamity Mary's right hand. Red smoke rose from the long black barrel. It was clearly no ordinary gun. Magic, maybe? Her sword-wielding hand was still numb.

Top Speed inserted herself between the two and spread her hands to both sides.

"Please, sis! Peace! Newbies always need to be taught respect! I'll scold her later, so please put down that gun. I'm begging ya!" she shouted in Mary's direction, then whispered to Ripple, "And you, put that away. Someone could get hurt!"

Calamity Mary spun her pistol before dropping it into its holster, and Ripple returned her sword to her back. Top Speed gave a sigh of relief.

"Peace, girls. Peace. We're all magical girls here, right? Comrades?"

Ripple didn't know what Calamity Mary was thinking, but she doubted she'd holstered her gun because they were comrades like Top Speed had suggested. She didn't consider Mary a comrade, and most likely the feeling was mutual.

"Well, all right. I'll yell at Fav later." And with that, Calamity Mary grabbed on to the guardrail and flipped over it with ease. At that moment, Ripple's heart pounded again—in the other girl's hand was a pistol, aimed at her. She'd totally missed the draw.

Multiple shots rang out. One bullet flew toward Top Speed while two flew toward her. Ripple grabbed her mentor by the collar and forced her down, simultaneously drawing her sword again and deflecting the bullets from a crouch. She came back up ready to retaliate with the throwing knives hidden in her sheath, but Calamity Mary was already gone.

"You two, I swear."

Top Speed stood herself up, rubbing her nose and forehead like she'd hit them.

"Why're ya so quick to pull the trigger? Have some damn restraint! Ever heard of it?"

"If someone picks a fight...you have to retaliate..."

"Well, learn to choose your battles! If you go starting shit every time she gets on your nerves, you won't live long!"

Ripple clicked her tongue. She was rattled and upset—first, with Top Speed for doing nothing the entire time. Second, with Calamity Mary and her bizarre willingness to fire at others without hesitation. And third, with herself for her terror at facing a gun, despite her tough act. She couldn't stand, her heart raced, and her sweat flowed like rivers, but somehow she barely managed not to cry.

Her right hand tingled from the impact of deflecting the bullets. When she'd become a magical girl and realized how strong she'd become, she had been so sure she couldn't be killed. Turns out she'd been wrong. Normal humans couldn't kill her. Most likely not even a disease or traffic accident could. But no matter how sturdy and resilient she was, another one like her could injure her. All of this made her angry.

"You're a sword with no sheath, like I used to be. Things could get bad if I left you alone. You could get up to some serious danger," Top Speed said, exasperated. That know-it-all look, those crossed arms, the lecturing—Ripple angrily clicked her tongue again.

Every evening after five o'clock, students packed into the hamburger shop in front of the train station and filled it with a thousand different conversations. The air bubbled with excitement and laughter, but the everyday chaos always stayed under control. The employees and customers were all used to it. Amid the hustle and bustle, three middle school girls occupying the three window seats near the door carried on their conversation like normal. One of them gestured at her smartphone and talked excitedly.

"The sightings are pouring in like crazy! See? Magical girls just have to exist!"

"Sumi…are you still going on about this?"

"Not even you can deny it when there are so many witness reports, Yocchan! They totally exist! So totally exist!"

"Of course I'll deny it. There's no freaking way."

"H-hey, Yocchan, why don't you believe in them?"

"You tell her, Koyuki! You speak for all the dreamers out there!"

"I dunno how to explain it. It's just plain embarrassing."

"Why is it embarrassing?"

"Wow, Koyuki, why're you so curious?"

"I just am!"

"Like, in anime and stuff, when a girl transforms there's a second where she's completely naked, right? It's like, are you an exhibitionist or something?"

"That doesn't happen! The media's lying to you!"

"Calm down, now. We're only talking about cartoons here, right?"

"Why are you two talking about anime, anyway? This stuff is happening in real life. There are eyewitnesses and everything."

"There's no way people can grow wings and fly or get hit by a dump truck and just walk it off."

"C'mon, Yocchan, dream a little. If something may or may not be real, it's just more fun to think it's real."

"Sumi, you need to come back to Earth. Reality is important."

"I'm not delusional, okay? I just think it would be cool if they existed, even if I know how reality works. Yocchan, you're missing out with that attitude. The Internet's going nuts! There's info on magical girls everywhere! My favorite's this one, the one in white. She seems real down-to-earth. I'd be relieved if she came to my rescue. She's, like, chicken soup for the soul."

"Koyuki, why are you grinning?"

"I-I'm not! I'm not grinning at all!"

◇◇◇

A week later—only seven days, and yet the anticipation had made them feel so long to Cranberry. A glance at any aggregate site revealed just how hard the other girls had been working. None of them wanted to be cut. Cranberry navigated to the chat on her magical phone and logged in.

Attendance was unusually high, similar to last time. Right away, Nemurin was unceremoniously named as the one among them with the least magical candy. She didn't seem particularly tortured or regretful about the results, just a little embarrassed. While the vast majority of the girls wanted to wield the great power they'd been given, she preferred to listen to their tales of adventure. Cranberry couldn't recall a week where Nemurin hadn't been there, and she was always easy to talk to.

But through her perfect attendance, her relationships with the others ran deep. Unlike Cranberry, simply there to be there, she had never missed an opportunity to chat or listen. Everyone knew her. Snow White, Top Speed, and Sister Nana were the most torn up about saying good-bye.

"I'll be watching you guys on the Internet. I'll always be cheering for you!"

To which Fav responded, "Well, good-bye, pon." And the pajama-wearing avatar was gone.

Then the top earner was also announced, which ended up being Snow White by a landslide.

"Everyone, try to emulate Snow White, pon," Fav said, ending the chat. One by one the girls left, until it was just Fav and Cranberry. She had a question she wanted answered.

Cranberry: I have one question, if you don't mind
Fav: What is it, pon?
Cranberry: What exactly happens when one loses the right to be a magical girl?

Fav: Girls who have been cut die, pon
Cranberry: Do you mean that figuratively? As in, they die as magical girls?
Fav: It's a biological death, pon

A franker answer there wasn't. Cranberry logged out without responding and tossed her magical phone at her pillow, just as she had a week ago. Chat logs were available even to those not present, which meant soon all the magical girls would learn what she and Fav had discussed. This would fundamentally change the implication of "getting the ax," not to mention the meaning of the game they were playing. Cranberry crossed her hands behind her head and rolled onto the bed, staring up at the ceiling.

CHAPTER 2
THE PRINCESS AND HER FOUR FOLLOWERS

Magical girls weren't so different from normal humans, in terms of their species. They were human, and humans could become magical girls. But the ones who made that leap could no longer be compared with normal people. Magic allowed them to draw forth exponentially more power.

"To lose the right to become a magical girl is to lose one's essence as a living being. In other words, death, pon."

"But that's exactly the problem! I'd rather go back to being normal than die!"

"Complain all you like, there's nothing that can be done now, pon."

"Nothing that can be done?!"

"Magical girls are natural-born warriors—their destiny is to fight, pon. Unflinching in the face of danger, they use brains, courage, and magic to overcome any crisis. The stronger the foe, the greater the joy—"

Snow White shut off her magical phone, abruptly ending her conversation with Fav. A few days ago she'd read through the logs and found the conversation between Cranberry and the mascot, which had led to a never-ending argument that only spun its wheels. When she said she'd rather quit than die, Fav revealed that if she quit she'd die anyway.

"You should have warned us!"

"No one forced you to pick up the game."

On and on the argument stretched. They were like two parallel lines, never meeting in the middle.

Snow White sighed. She couldn't tell anyone what she was. Doing so would mean she'd forfeit her powers and die. She couldn't even tell her parents or friends her life would end, or she'd perish on the spot.

Two days after the chat, a small blurb in the obituary section of the local newspaper revealed that a twenty-four-year-old female, one Nemu Sanjou, had passed. Her time of death was the time the chat had ended, and the cause of death was a sudden heart attack despite no history of illness. All these factors led to one conclusion. It had to have been Nemurin.

We're really...gonna die.

Snow White sighed again, then gazed out at the horizon. With her magically improved eyesight, she could see every detail of the ocean, even from atop the steel tower. Dozens of fishing boats were setting out for the open ocean. *They get to be so carefree, and I have to deal with this.* She felt an unreasonable anger inside, but knowing it was irrational just made her depressed.

I've just been worrying about myself. I'm putting my own life above Nemurin's death. We talked so much, and we were such good friends, but after some crying and a night's sleep all I can think about is myself. I feel guilty. I'm scared to die. My stomach hurts. I wanna throw up. But I don't wanna die. I don't wanna die. I don't wanna die. I don't wanna die. I'm scared to die.

An electronic beeping brought her back to reality. Next to her was La Pucelle, fiddling with her magical device.

"What are you doing?"

She heard a noise like a level-up chime from an RPG.

"Mind checking your magical phone for me?"

"Sure, but…what are you doing?"

She turned on her phone and checked the screen. Displayed were the time, humidity, temperature, her magical candy total…

"Huh?"

Assuming her memory wasn't off, she'd had more candy the previous night. Yet somehow her total had been cut in half.

"Wait, what the heck happened? Oh my gosh!"

"Calm down. I'll send them back."

Again came the level-up sound, and Snow White's candy total was the same as she remembered.

"What is this?"

"Fav told us there'd been an update to the magical phones. They added the ability to share magical candy. You can do it even if the other phone is off. It takes a little while to complete the transfer, though."

"Oh… So?"

"It's probably Fav's way of telling us to work together to get more candy, considering the timing of the update."

Snow White studied the knight sitting next to her. Even with the cold and cloudy night sky as a background, her face was noble and beautiful—and just a little bit excited.

"Sou, are you gonna go get candy?"

"Stop calling me Sou. And if I don't gather candy I'm gonna get the ax, literally. So it's better than nothing."

"You're not scared or anything?"

"Are you scared, Snow White?"

"Sure I am. I don't want to let anyone else die, or die myself. Then I wouldn't be able to see my parents, my friends, I wouldn't be able to watch magical-girl anime, eat good food, see cool stuff, laugh…"

"I know it's scary. I'm scared, too. Who wouldn't be?"

La Pucelle's expression hardened. Startled, Snow White tried to distance herself, but La Pucelle placed a hand on hers. Snow White swallowed, finding herself unable to reject her.

"But if we let the fear paralyze us, it'll be us on the chopping block next. You don't want that, do you? So let's work hard together."

She would have been right at home with the girls on TV she'd cheered for all those years—ready to challenge even the strongest enemy with a heart determined to protect those important to her. Were the others thinking the same thing? Were they steeling their resolves, just as La Pucelle had? Snow White felt like the odd one out for being so scared. Was she the strange one? What would Nemurin say? Snow White recalled her smiling face, all ears to yet another story of adventure. She wiped her eyes with her sleeve.

"Don't cry, Snow White."

La Pucelle drew her sword from its sheath, offered the handle to her, and took a knee. The blade was nearly two feet long, its steel sparkling.

"My sworn friend Snow White, I vow to be your sword, no matter what befalls me."

Her words and actions seemed rehearsed, but her eyes were sincere. Despite being told not to cry, Snow White couldn't suppress the great big tears spilling forth. She hugged La Pucelle tightly and put her lips to her ear.

"Thank you..."

Sensing the warmth of La Pucelle's body, her face began to burn. She glanced at her friend, whose cheeks also seemed to burn a deep shade of red.

◇◇◇

Ripple had no idea what Top Speed liked about her, but she was acutely aware of her new title—partner. In chat, the witch went on about "my partner this" and "my partner that" and then made sure to let Ripple know, even though she never asked. It annoyed her. The only sounds from her mouth were tongue clicks. But the ninja never turned her away or yelled at, abused, or hit her, instead choosing to let her talk. Top Speed, taking Ripple's silence as approval, showed up almost daily to pick her up for a night of candy gathering. But Ripple hadn't simply caved. She wouldn't be putting herself through hell for no good reason.

Ripple's pinpoint accurate shuriken only helped those in need if they were in a very dangerous situation, and those didn't happen every day. Ripple's only recourse was to use her enhanced physical abilities, something any other magical girl could do. She had no special advantage.

Top Speed, on the other hand, had the unique ability of flight, thanks to her magic broomstick, Rapid Swallow. This was far more useful than Ripple's ability to throw things. It wasn't a matter of helping people more easily—it was much easier to search from the skies for chances to lend a hand.

When she heard about Nemurin's death, Top Speed raged and cried. Ripple, however, calmly considered what actions to take in the future. Of course, she couldn't deny she was angry at the mysterious force putting her life in danger, and the fear of death was so painful she wanted to clutch at her chest to suppress it. But still, she did her best to remain calm. She had to gather candy like her life depended on it, because it literally did. Everything that could be used, should be used. If Top Speed provided a unique advantage, she had no choice but to put up with the irritation in silence.

From Rapid Swallow's rear seat, she zoomed around her designated area earning points. Top Speed's dedication to survival was greater than expected. "I can't die," she'd declared to Ripple with an oddly serious expression. The silence she got in response had prompted an addendum. "I just need at least another six months," she'd whispered. Ripple questioned this oddly specific amount of time, but Top Speed simply smiled wryly and didn't answer. She wrote it off as more babbling.

"So today we'll be flying along the national highway, okay?"

"Roger..."

"I wish there was a place we could earn a little more points, though."

Ripple had suggested the red-light district would be more

profitable, but the largest one in the city was in the Jounan district. That was Calamity Mary's territory, and Top Speed had firmly rejected the idea. Ripple had questioned her lack of dedication, considering they could die if they failed, but Top Speed insisted it made no sense to put themselves in danger when the goal was to live longer. In the end, they settled on making do with the districts they'd been assigned.

Nakayado and Kitayado had respectable populations, but the militaristic air of their castle-town days was long gone. Truthfully, the people were quite mellow. This was not a bad thing—in fact, she preferred this—but that naturally came with a lower number of opportunities to assist.

The two of them stayed up all night searching for problems to solve, even skipping meals, and generally kept quite busy. Of course, once a magical girl was transformed, hunger and fatigue became nonfactors. But above all, they didn't want to die.

While "annoying but useful, thus worth putting up with" was Ripple's appraisal of Top Speed, something she'd obviously never say out loud, she couldn't help but raise that evaluation a little every time they landed on the roof of the Seventh Sankou building after a ride on her magic broomstick.

Since each girl had her own unique ability, forming a team with trustworthy people was the best way to gather candy efficiently. But for Ripple, who preferred to be alone and had always avoided contact with her colleagues other than Top Speed, this was no easy task.

For this reason, Top Speed flew in two more of their number. With her wide network of connections as a regular chat attendee, it was no surprise she knew a few who could be trusted not to stab them in the back, at least.

The two introduced themselves as Sister Nana and Weiss Winterprison. Sister Nana's appearance was obviously that of a nun. Her costume resembled the traditional habit, especially the veil and long skirt, and her face had an air of kindness to it. Yet a

real nun would never allow a thigh-high slit on her skirt or wear a garter belt on top of white stockings. Ripple wondered if it was just magical-girl style to inspire lust with normally impossible combinations.

On first glance, Weiss Winterprison seemed to be a man. Her brown hair was trimmed short, and she was a head taller than Ripple. A coat covered in belts, almost like a straitjacket, draped over her body. The scarf around her neck was so long it dangled by her feet, and she used it to hide her mouth. Her austere garb was colored black from head to foot, and while her face was beautiful, as befitting a magical heroine, it was an androgynous beauty. The coat around her hid all signs of feminine lines. She most strongly resembled a prince of a foreign country.

"It's good to meet you, Ripple. I am Sister Nana. Pleasure to make your acquaintance. This is Weiss Winterprison."

"Hi."

Sister Nana spoke softly, which to Ripple meant she was slow of mind. Winterprison's voice was low, her demeanor curt. To Ripple, this was a sign of a superiority complex. Neither made an incredible first impression, but then again, no one had ever made a good first impression on Ripple. That wasn't hugely concerning. What was concerning was Top Speed's troubled expression as she dropped them off. After a few more formalities, Sister Nana began.

"I think this is wrong."

She got straight to the point.

"What's wrong?"

"This situation. We were given power to bring peace to the world of man, not to hate, quarrel, and compete among ourselves. What good can this accomplish?"

She clasped Ripple's hands and drew closer. Ripple frowned, but the nun paid her no mind and continued.

"It is during times like these that we must band together."

"Yeah, but what exactly are we supposed to do?" Top Speed asked in Ripple's stead. Sister Nana turned her head to face the witch, her hands still gripping Ripple's, and smiled gently.

"That is what we should first consider. If we put our minds together, we can surely come up with a sound idea."

Top Speed grinned awkwardly, Ripple tsked, and Winterprison coughed. It was entirely possible the cough was meant as a warning to Ripple for clicking her tongue, but either way, Sister Nana continued unfazed.

"Only the mind of a magical girl can solve this. I submitted a formal complaint to the management through Fav, but it was ignored."

"Oh, you did?"

"Yes, but it did no good. Fav told me to give up because that's just how things are… But this is not an issue we can afford to give up on! One poor soul has already fallen victim to this vicious system. Nemurin… What regret, what sadness, what pain she must have felt… The poor thing."

A single tear spilled from Sister Nana's eye. Ripple clicked her tongue. Just like the class president she'd had in second grade, Sister Nana expected people to flock to her side by spouting pretty words. Just like her seventh grade homeroom teacher, she pitied others in order to think of herself as kind. Just like…well, many women, but her mother most of all, she felt no shame in crying.

She also didn't seem to be proposing they work together to gather candy.

Ripple wrested her hands free from Sister Nana, sending her toppling into Winterprison's arms. The nun's shoulders quivered as Winterprison held her close.

"Oh… The poor soul…"

Behind Sister Nana, Winterprison glowered at Ripple, her eyes ablaze with anger. The gesture was returned with murderous intent. The taller girl narrowed her glare, and Ripple moistened her lips. Winterprison stepped in front of Sister Nana as if to protect her. The ninja moved her right hand to her back and found the hilt of her sword.

"All right! I see what you're trying to say!" Top Speed shouted, and clapped her hands loudly, attempting to dispel the tension. "I need to discuss things with my partner, so let's leave it at that for today. Okay?"

"We need to act fast to prevent any more victims—"

"Yeah, I know. Understood! Which is exactly why we want to talk things over first. We know how important this is, and that's why we don't want to decide lightly."

Sister Nana seemed unsatisfied but grudgingly nodded, and the two girls hopped on Top Speed's broom and zipped away. Upon her equally rushed return, Top Speed put her hands together and bowed deeply to Ripple.

"Sorry."

"Go to hell."

"Seriously, I'm sorry. They just said they wanted to talk, so I was like, why not? I didn't think you'd get so pissed. And on the off chance they had a good idea, why not go along with it? I really don't want to die either. At least not for six months."

Why was she so insistent on six months? Ripple clicked her tongue. How many times had she done that today?

"So irritating…"

"It's not like they meant any harm, y'know? You guys just didn't gel, I guess. Don't go starting any fights here. No way I'm gonna let myself die. I'm not getting caught up in some brawl between you and Winterprison."

It seemed to Ripple that Top Speed's insistence on survival wasn't because she was simply afraid of dying. *Six months, huh? What's in six months?*

Ripple pointed at Top Speed.

"Your back…"

"Hmm?"

"It says 'No Gratuitous Opinions.'"

"Oh…"

"You have no spine…"

"Yeesh, you're harsh. I really don't recommend fighting Winterprison, though. Remember what I said before? Apparently she saved Sister Nana from Calamity Mary by tackling her head-on. Sister Nana told me all about it with a little blush."

Ripple remembered Sister Nana's tears as she lay in Winter-prison's arms and scowled. That they didn't "gel" wasn't even the half of it. The point was Nana's plan wouldn't do any good.

"She's not a bad person.".

"Delusional religious fanatics disgust me…"

"I don't think she's exactly delusional. More like rotten, I think. Well, either way, we're back to patrolling the roads for candy."

"We'll still need to defend ourselves…"

"We can just run away. I'm the fastest in town, y'know. They don't call me Top Speed for nothing. I'll always leave the rear seat open so I can swoop down and rescue ya. No one'll ever catch us. That's why I'm playing this game fair and square. I'll keep watch from the skies and intervene when something happens. That should be enough to land us tons of candy."

Ripple knew any further discussion would only prove fruit-less, so she silently sat behind Top Speed and wrapped her hands around her waist.

◇◇◇

N City's Nishimonzen was crowded with temples. From grand, enormous structures to tiny ones tucked away in between build-ings, shrines lined the streets. And of all the temples in Nishi-monzen, Ouketsuji was the oldest—or rather, the most decrepit. It was not some ancient and storied place, and it had no one to look after it. It had simply been left to rot. And as far as the middle of town went, it wasn't a bad place to hide magical girls. Specifically, five of them.

Ruler fingered her tiara, then adjusted its position and sat down, using her long cape as a cushion.

"As you know, our magical phones have received an update."

As she spoke, Ruler focused on a decapitated statue of a bodhi-sattva. Kneeling there was a girl in swimwear. Ruler found her-self thinking that if the pure white school swimsuit and goggles dangling from her neck reflected her identity as a swimmer, then the headphones and curls were pointless additions serving as her magical-girl chic. The swimsuit meant for younger kids combined with that voluptuous body made for a morally indecent picture.

"This update allows us to move magical candy between us."

A few feet in front of her was a girl with doglike ears, only her head visible above the hole in the dirt floor. According to her, she felt most at home in holes she dug herself. She wore a hooded cape, and her dog ears peeked out from holes on the top. Paw gloves covered her hands, and around her neck hung a collar. The patches of fur on her outfit and tights were white with black polka dots, and her shorts had a hole in them near her butt to allow her tail to poke through.

"Does everyone understand what this means?"

Perched on a beam was a crow wearing a ruby necklace. The next second, it was a black cat in boots. The second after that, two magical girls sat in its place, swan-like wings on their backs and rings of light above their heads. Despite their many forms, this was their true one. They appeared to be ten years old. Their dresses and headbands were a matching navy blue, their blouses and drawers white, perfectly matched like members of a choir. There were only two ways to tell the girls apart: whether their short bobbed hair flipped under or out, and whether the ribbon each wore around her ankle was on the left or right.

"Those who have lots of candy should share with those who don't?"

The dog-eared Tama cocked her head and made a suggestion, to which Ruler responded coldly, "Zero points."

"We should form teams and try to make sure we all have enough candy?" "Oh, that sounds right. Sis, you're so magi-cool."

The twin angels Minael and Yunael, known as the Peaky Angels, pointed at each other.

"Thirty points," Ruler announced. "Swim Swim, what do you think?"

The girl dressed for the pool, Swim Swim, said not a word but shook her head. Her sizable breasts shook in unison with her head. Ruler spat silently. She was not particularly endowed, neither as a regular human nor in her transformed state, and had a considerable complex about it.

"I'm surrounded by idiots." She glared at them all. "Idiots, every last one of you."

The Peaky Angels looked away, Tama lowered her ears apologetically, and Swim Swim continued to stare at Ruler without moving. They weren't the only idiots Ruler was referring to, however. Every last magical girl running around to help others in an effort to save themselves after Nemurin's death was an idiot.

"This is a message from the management. They're telling us to steal from each other."

"What? We're allowed to steal?" "Really?"

"We don't need anyone's permission. We can just take their magical phone and perform the transfer ourselves. I've already tried it."

"Seriously?" "That's amazing."

"If all you're capable of is kissing ass, then shut up, you obnoxious idiots."

The twin angels once again averted their eyes. Ruler snorted, then continued.

"I'm going to have you follow my orders. Work hard if you don't want to end up like Nemurin."

"Orders?" "What are you going to make us do?"

She wanted to yell at them for trying to kiss ass again, but Ruler decided it was more important to proceed than to give the twins a tongue-lashing.

"Simple. We'll steal from the one with the most candy: Snow White."

Sanae Mokuou had been so happy to become a magical girl and finally attain the greatness she deserved. She'd gone to highly acclaimed elementary and middle schools, then it was high school, university, and straight into employment at a top-class company. All the while, she had been surrounded by idiots. She constantly wondered why she was forced to work with morons who couldn't understand her value, and she even said so out loud. Because of that, she had no friends and had spent her whole life alone.

She'd picked up *Magical Girl Raising Project* as a pastime, and when she transformed, she finally had a clear answer to her eternal question of why all the stupid people around her couldn't recognize her worth: She was the ugly duckling. Though she was a swan among them, none of the ducks appreciated her beauty. That day, Sanae quit her job.

The heroine in the mirror filled her with pride. Her lustrous satin cloak, encrusted with jewels, flowed all the way to the floor; an eagle with a jewel in its claws topped her yard-long ivory scepter; and long gloves fit for a party and a tiara finished off the set. The tiara was small and simple in design, but the diamond embedded in it was of unnatural size and clarity. Ornaments held her regal purple updo in place, while her feet rested in glass slippers. Her eyelashes were so long you could almost hear them when she blinked. She had no need for foundation or makeup. She was free of all the miscellaneous chores she'd hated as a normal human. Now she could join her fellow swans. But Sanae's joy vanished when she met her mentor, Calamity Mary.

The other girl smoked a cigar, blowing the smoke in Sanae's face, and knocked back her bottle of booze at regular intervals. The minute Sanae decided she'd had enough of her delinquency and stood up to leave, a gunshot rang out, and an explosive roar boomed from behind her. She turned to see a hole nearly ten feet wide in the wall behind her.

"Do not go against me. Do not give me trouble. Do not piss me off. Okay?"

Sanae was frozen, half sitting, half standing.

"Okay?"

At some point, Calamity Mary's gun had made it to her hand. The only explanation for the hole in the wall was that a bullet from that gun had created it. But no pistol was capable of such results.

"Is this…your magic?"

"Why are you asking me that? I asked you a question first, little girl, so answer. Nod like an idiot if you have to. Okay?"

After a long, long time, Sanae nodded deeply.

"Okay, okay. Good answer."

Her quick draw was fearsome. Sanae hadn't even seen her take out her weapon, let alone cock the hammer or fire. By the time the wall had exploded, everything was over.

Calamity Mary blew away the smoke trailing from the barrel of the gun with a quick puff, spun it a few times, then holstered it in one smooth motion. Then she tilted back her bottle of booze and gulped loudly. The amber liquid dripped from the corner of her lips and splashed onto her breasts.

Sanae's blood boiled from the humiliation, and she bit her lip. She'd been powerless, cowed by violence. She understood her own magic, of course, and was satisfied with its strength, but Calamity Mary completely outclassed her in speed. If she tried to use magic on her, she was more likely to end up with a hole in her, just like the wall. She understood her own body. While it wasn't as fragile as a wall, the best she could hope for was a critical injury—at worst, she'd die instantly. Basically, she was no different from a normal human facing a normal gun.

The moment she thought she'd become a swan, her head had been grabbed and shoved underwater. Sanae chewed on the humiliation and learned her lesson. What she needed were bodyguards, she realized—human shields that could withstand punishment until she could cast her magic on Calamity Mary and exact her revenge. Thus, every time a new girl joined, she volunteered whenever she could to be their mentor, solicited the easily manipulated ones, and formed her own faction. It consisted of the slow-headed Tama; the Peaky Angels, who blindly followed any and all orders; and the taciturn Swim Swim.

Tama was a dog, a foolishly faithful creature who obeyed a strong owner. No matter how many times she was beaten or kicked, she would continue to wag her tail happily for her master. When Sanae gave her a collar, she joyously ran laps around the temple.

The Peaky Angels were cowards. One strong word from her rendered them speechless. Sanae still had no idea which was Yunael and which was Minael, but they'd never made a fuss about it.

Swim Swim's silence stemmed from ignorance. Sanae had once discovered her staring at a Nishimonzen directory sign. When she asked why, the girl had responded with, "What does this mean?" while pointing at the English letters of "Nishimonzen." She remembered everything she was told, so it wasn't that she had terrible memory, but she often couldn't read simple kanji, either. They did say women with big breasts were stupid, though.

All of her followers were idiots. None of them could think and act on their own. But by following Sanae's orders, they could do something of significance. They were happier this way, even if they had to die for her.

The Peaky Angels agreed to the candy theft strategy easily, saying, "Sure, that's easier." "Super-cool, huh?" and Swim Swim nodded silently, but Tama was the only one who couldn't get past the ethical problem—should magical girls be stealing from others?

"You have to listen to what the leader says," Swim Swim warned, and in the end Tama, too, nodded.

Ruler had a rough understanding of Snow White's usual patterns, but to confirm that nothing had changed recently, she sent out Tama and the Peaky Angels to scout. Only she and Swim Swim stayed behind at Ouketsuji. Ruler found herself repeatedly glancing at Swim Swim, sitting on her knees and not moving a muscle. She just wouldn't move, so finally Ruler opened her mouth.

"Why are you on your knees?"

"This is the proper position to assume when before our honored leader."

"...Is that something I told you?"

"Yes."

She had a habit of reciting Ruler's past instructions at every opportunity. She remembered everything, even the meaningless insults and thoughtless narcissistic declarations Ruler had forgotten herself. She had accepted Swim Swim's behavior as simple loyalty, but there were times that it wore on her.

"*Just as you may not tell regular humans your true identity, you may not share it with other magical girls without my permission.*"

"*Your leader must be the object of your affection. The organization is most effective when everyone tries to imitate her.*"

"*Above all, deal with strong enemies swiftly.*"

"*Never let down your guard, even after becoming a magical girl and gaining mystical powers. If any enemies that can fight us exist, they, too, will have similar powers.*"

Sometimes she'd run her mouth based on whatever was happening at the time, but Swim Swim remembered it all. Ruler walked over to her, crouched down, and patted her head.

"Even an idiot can be slightly bearable if she fills her head with noble things."

"Noble things like what?"

Ruler smiled and answered, her voice cold as ice.

"My words."

Ruler's strategy was simple. It had to be, or her brainless subordinates would fail to keep up, make stupid mistakes, and bungle the entire operation. They would attack the Kubegahama steel tower where La Pucelle and Snow White met—before they could join forces. She knew they met up there because they'd left discussions mentioning the fact in the chat log. "My idiots aren't the only ones, it seems," she'd gloated when she found the logs.

But just because they met there didn't mean they arrived at the same time. There was a small window when one would be alone. If La Pucelle arrived first, the Peaky Angels and Tama would attack and attempt to delay her. Then, when Snow White showed up, Ruler and Swim Swim would attack and steal her candy. If Snow White arrived first, the order would be reversed.

Ruler had no experience in battles between magical girls. Nor did she have any information on what kind of special powers they'd be up against. It was concerning, but the same went for her opponents. Most likely neither La Pucelle nor Snow White had ever fought another of their kind before, and no one knew what magic Ruler's group was capable of. Tama's ability to instantly dig holes was well suited to ambushes, and the Peaky Angels' abilities to transform and fly were perfect for diversions. Ruler's magic was unbeatable as long as she had a guard, which made Swim Swim perfect for the job, since she could nullify physical attacks with her magic. As a team, they weren't too shabby.

As long as the idiots don't make stupid mistakes...

Then the magical candy theft would be a success.

This would be a practice run, a test of sorts. If they succeeded, they could move on to the next step: assaulting Calamity Mary and stealing her candy. Ruler's humiliation still smoldered, and its embers would never be extinguished until Calamity Mary was on her knees.

"There!" "I see La Pucelle!"

The Peaky Angels reported through their devices. Apparently, they had spotted La Pucelle from their vantage point above.

"She's running toward the tower!" "She's pretty fast with all that armor!"

"Execute the plan accordingly."

Swim Swim and Ruler leaped from the bushes beneath the steel tower and began to ascend.

La Pucelle slowed when she noticed the two angels descending upon her.

Yunael and Minael together formed the Peaky Angels. She'd seen them in chat before, but never in real life. The sneers on their faces half explained what was going on, but their next action—simultaneous dive kicks from the front and back—made their intentions perfectly clear. She dived off the gravel path and rolled over some bushes, drew her sword from its sheath, and, still crouched, pointed its tip at the twin angels. With one hand she easily wielded the two-and-a-half-foot blade, stopping it on a dime.

"What do you want?"

"'What do you want?' she asks!" "Isn't it obvious?" "Candy, please!"

Her blood boiled with anger at the magical girls so weak-willed that they instantly turned to stealing others' hard-earned reward—and just a tiny bit of excitement at the opportunity to unleash her full power. Ever since she'd obtained this strength, she'd dreamed of victory over a powerful enemy.

The twin angels flapped their body-length wings and circled from above. They seemed to be looking for the right moment to strike. They'd definitely attack as soon as she tried to stand. La Pucelle slowly moved her left hand, then stopped. Something was vibrating ever so slightly.

Below!

Just as the circling angels rocketed toward La Pucelle, a three-foot-wide hole opened up below her. If she didn't jump, the opening would swallow her, but if she did jump, the angels would attack her while she was unable to move freely in the air. Both choices would lead her to a worst-case scenario—so she chose neither. Instantly she reacted, jamming her sword beneath her feet and jumping on it. Width, length, and thickness all grew to five times the original size, until the sword could support La Pucelle and keep her from falling into the hole.

This was La Pucelle's magic: to change the size of her sword at will. She could choose the perfect length for any moment. She could hear scratching from within the hole, but it was impossible to nick the enchanted sword.

Hesitation flashed across the angels' faces. They tried to stop their descent, but instead they lost their balance in midair. Noticing this, La Pucelle leaped off her sword and swung her sheath at one of the angels.

The angel tried to dodge, but was surprised when she couldn't. She had thought she was far enough away, but failed to account for the sheath's newly gigantic size as well. The sword wasn't the only thing that could expand—the sheath covering it was also capable of this. Its flat side connected, smacking the angel to the ground. La Pucelle landed and dashed toward the hole, shrinking her sword to a little under two feet. With the cover on the hole gone, someone appeared from inside it.

"Hey, what the heck—"

Tama popped her head out of the ground, sensing something was amiss, and La Pucelle attacked without mercy. The solid kick to her temple sent Tama flying straight back into the hole with a muffled grunt. Their formation broken, La Pucelle picked up her sword and turned to face her last enemy.

"What do you want?"

She repeated the question she'd asked when they first attacked, but the angel was gone. All she could see was a single crow cocking its head at her. La Pucelle glanced back at the angel she'd brought down, but no one was there, either—just a rubber ball. Before she could figure out what was happening, the crow took flight, picked up the ball, and flew off toward the steel tower. Their forms stretched, bent, morphed, and changed color until they were no longer a crow and ball, but two angels.

Transformation? Is that their magic?

"That's good enough of a diversion, right, sis?" "Yeah! No problemo!"

A diversion?

La Pucelle looked up at the top of the steel tower. She could see one, two, three silhouettes—clearly Snow White was not alone up there. Her boiling blood chilled in an instant.

"Damn it!"

She cursed loudly—unbecoming of a gallant knight—and ran up the tower after the two angels.

Meanwhile, the plan went perfectly for Ruler and Swim Swim. They'd scaled the steel tower and attacked the magical girl standing there—the one in the white school uniform, and the darling of Internet news sites. Without a doubt, she was Snow White. Her face twisted in fright as she looked from Ruler to Swim Swim.

"Wh-what?" she asked, voice quavering. She looked and sounded more like a civilian than a fighter, a victim more than a perpetrator. Clearly, she had no intent to fight.

Fool, do you still not realize what I'm here for? Or do you just not want to fight, even knowing what I want? Either way, you're a fool, Ruler venomously thought to herself. She raised her staff—her royal scepter—pointed it at Snow White, and made her magical decree.

"In the name of Ruler, I order you, Snow White, not to move."

Snow White froze as she prepared to run, her face still taut with fear. Swim Swim took out her phone, aimed it at Snow White, and began the candy transfer.

This was Ruler's magic—the ability to make others obey her decrees.

Her power had a few rules. She had to point her scepter at them and strike a pose. She had to hold the pose to keep the decree active. She had to say, "In the name of Ruler." She could not be more than fifteen feet from the person. And she could have a maximum of four people under her command. However, such an ability was powerful enough to require such limitations. Once she made her decree, it was checkmate.

The Peaky Angels, Tama, and Swim Swim weren't aware that she had restrictions. She'd merely explained that her magic allowed her to order others around. She wasn't foolish enough to tell her subordinates her own weaknesses. It was much more convenient for them to think of her as an all-powerful leader.

The decree "give me your candy" would have been less complicated than "do not move," but it didn't prevent the problem of an immediate counterattack once the candy was transferred, so she prioritized safety. Ruler was clever, and clever people were careful.

"Swim Swim, are you done yet?"

"Almost."

"Honestly. This pose is tiring, you know."

"Just a little more and I'll be—"

Swim Swim cut off. Ruler looked to where she was gazing, and down below them, two angels hurtled toward the tower. Behind them she could see a knight charging through the gravel and leaving a cloud of dust in her wake.

"Those stupid, idiotic, garbage... They couldn't even manage to be a distraction?"

"I'm almost done."

"Shut up, fool!"

Snow White was under attack. Images of her crying and afraid—and finally of the human Koyuki Himekawa—popped into La Pucelle's head. She felt like her heart was being ripped in two, but at least the blood that had been pounding angrily in her head was now circulating through her body.

To La Pucelle—Souta Kishibe—a magical girl was a heroine who fought. He had no problems with the old-school ones who solved problems around the neighborhood, but to him they were warriors who stood bravely in the face of giant enemies and never gave up protecting what was important to them.

At the top of the steel tower, Snow White needed rescue. However, if La Pucelle just ran straight up, the flying duo was sure to attack her. If the Peaky Angels had completely lost the will to fight, that would be one thing, but from the looks on their faces as they glanced back occasionally, they weren't exactly running in fear. She'd be forced into a two-on-one midair battle if they attacked while she scaled the steel tower with no stable footing. Even if she did win, it would only help them with their goal of stalling for time. Her opponents had the numbers and the terrain advantage—the fight probably wouldn't be over quickly. For all the exhilaration she felt at finally being able to unleash her full power, she was acutely aware of her limits. *I really am a natural-born warrior*, she gloated, but soon snapped herself out of it. She didn't have many options to save Snow White.

In the few seconds before she reached the tower, La Pucelle observed, thought, found a solution, and acted on it—she charged at the tower with everything she had and shoulder-tackled one of its legs with all her momentum, weight, and power.

From below, the tower's shaking seemed violent, but at the top it was far worse. The power lines snapped and flailed in the air. They felt like they could almost touch the ground, the shuddering was so violent. Ruler, posing with her scepter, and Snow White, forbidden to move, lost their balance and were hurled from the top. Swim Swim, also falling from the tower, grabbed Ruler's hand and threw her high into the air, where the twin angels caught her.

Meanwhile, La Pucelle raced to intercept Snow White's deadly plunge. She caught her, and the two tumbled about thirty feet before finally stopping in some bushes.

Ruler glared angrily at Snow White and La Pucelle, dangling by the arms between the Peaky Angels. They had saved her from the fall, but the position was hardly elegant and only infuriated her. Swim Swim, on the other hand, had no one to save her and would hit the ground. Luckily, her magic would allow her to nullify the damage. Once they all grouped up, they'd be four against two. As Ruler thought about this, she remembered something.

"Where's Tama?"

"La Pucelle kicked her and that was it." "Dunno if she's alive or dead."

This was the same knight who had managed to shake the giant steel tower, nearly toppling it or even breaking it. It wasn't hard to imagine one blow taking Tama out of commission. So, considering the fact that Tama and the Peaky Angels had roundly lost in a three-on-one...

"Okay, let's retreat."

"Huh?" "Seriously?"

"It's a strategic retreat! Stop blathering and about-face right!"

As Snow White and La Pucelle picked themselves up, the

angels made their escape with a sharp turn to the right, leaving the pair behind.

Ultimately, the cowardly-seeming strategic retreat turned out to be correct. Tama had made her way back to Ouketsuji on her own. Her memories were a bit scrambled, but then again her brain was normally scrambled, so Ruler deemed it not a problem. Swim Swim had not just returned, but returned victoriously after completing her task—she'd succeeded in stealing Snow White's magical candy and come home in style. Her magical candy stores, formerly 826 pieces, had jumped to 2,914 pieces after the operation. She had taken 2,088 pieces, which was more than anyone in their group, including Ruler, possessed by a factor of two.

"She collected 2,000 pieces on her own?" "How do you even get that many?" "So bourgeois." "This is a modern-day revolution!" "Sis, you're so magi-cool."

"Uhhh, so what do we do with the candy?"

"We snagged 2,088." "Divided by five, that's 417, remainder three. It's uneven."

"Yuna-Minael, you're so good at math!"

"No, there's no remainder."

Their math had been correct, but they'd used the wrong equation, so Ruler corrected them.

"826 from 2,914 gives 2,088. So far, you're correct."

"The rest is wrong?" "How?"

"What makes you think we're splitting it evenly? 2,088 divided by two is 1,044, which goes to me, the leader. The other half we divide by two again, which is 522. That's Swim Swim's share. 522 divided by three is 174. Yunael, Minael, Tama, that's your share. See? Perfect."

The run-down temple went silent. The hushed stillness, which should have been normal for the abandoned temple, was eerie. Ruler immediately broke the silence she had created.

"Anyone have something to say?" She glared. "We have you incapable idiots, who couldn't even do the job you were given, a

helpful idiot who actually managed to fulfill her task, and me, the leader—creator of the plan and executor of its most important role. So what would make you think we get equal rewards? Are you stupid? Oh, yes, you are. I knew that. You're senseless, incapable, and can't even stall one person three-on-one. You almost screwed up the whole plan! But out of the kindness of my heart, I'll forget this."

Ruler pointed at each of them in turn and scowled. The twin angels looked away, Tama's ears drooped, and Swim Swim just listened, kneeling with perfect posture. Ruler snorted and jabbed her scepter into the temple ground.

"Know your place, idiots. Just be grateful you haven't been punished."

CHAT #2

Fav: Now it's time for this week's chat~

Fav: but it seems we're missing a few people today, pon

Fav: I hope they don't think they can just check the logs later, pon

Fav: No one here seems to be talking much either

Fav: so let's try to make this a little more bright and fun, pon

Fav: That's what magical girls are all about, pon ☆

Fav: Now, back on topic

Fav: Let's talk about something happier, pon

Fav: A new girl will be joining us this week~ Clappy clap~

Fav: Um… She doesn't appear to be here

Fav: She's probably just shy, pon

Fav: Still, please try to attend next week, okay?

Fav: Promise Fav, pon ☆

Fav: Next, what you're all most interested in…

Fav: Time to announce who has the least candy this week, pon

Fav: This week, it was…

Fav: Ruler

Fav: Hmm, too bad, pon

Fav: It looks like you tried really hard, but you just barely lost, pon

Fav: Hey, hey. Say all you like, Fav is in a pickle, too, pon

Fav: Oh, and this week's top earner was Snow White, pon
Fav: Congrats on two weeks straight~!
Fav: Everyone, gather lots of candy and aim for the top, pon
Fav: Well, see you all here next week, pon
Fav: Bye-bye~!

The chat ended—only Tama, Swim Swim, the Peaky Angels, Ruler, Cranberry, and Fav had been in attendance. Everyone was probably on high alert and considered the others their enemies.

"Man, that worked perfectly!" "So magi-cool, huh?"

The fading light illuminated the run-down temple grounds of Ouketsuji in Nishizenmon. The Peaky Angels weren't even attempting to hide their glee as they high-fived, clapped, and hugged. They paid Tama and Swim Swim no mind—the former's expression was mournful, while the latter displayed no emotion. This elicited more from the angels.

"The nasty girl is gone!" "Ms. I'm-better-than-you!" "Ms. I-won't-share-the-candy!" "Ms. You're-nothing-but-idiots-and-morons!" "Seriously, what a nasty girl."

To the Peaky Angels, Ruler had been nothing but terrible. She was haughty, greedy, and whenever she opened her mouth it was to insult or belittle. Had she known how Minael and Yunael had talked behind her back?

In Tama's eyes, Ruler had been a scary person. Her reasons were the same as the twin angels'.

But Swim Swim had known—to the three of them, on some level or another, Ruler was a hindrance. So much so that they would easily agree to getting rid of her.

"So, what do we do with this?" "Take it out into the mountains and bury it?" "It should be easy with your magic, Tama." "You can whip up a hole in no time."

Minael, Yunael, and Swim Swim were discussing the body of a perfectly ordinary young woman in her late twenties. She had on a cardigan over her pajamas and sandals on her feet.

"Do we really have to go to all that trouble, though?" "Oh, good point." "Let's just dump her somewhere in the middle of the night. Someone will find her in the morning." "Yeah, let's do that."

Ruler had screamed "Why?! How?!" until her very last breath. Even lying on the ground as a normal human, her hands were outstretched as if she were trying desperately to grab on to something.

Swim Swim stood up and went over to Tama, who was hugging her knees, covering her ears, and shivering. Bending down to her eye level, she soothed her with a pat on the head. Tears welled in Tama's eyes. Swim Swim relaxed her face, lifted the corner of her mouth slightly, and said simply, "It's okay." She patted the other girl on the head again. "I'll take care of the body," she declared, picking it up and slinging it over her shoulder.

"You don't have to do that, Swim." "Yeah, yeah. You're our new leader."

"We're disbanding. You're all free to do as you please."

Behind her the Peaky Angels still tried to argue, but Swim Swim ignored them and pushed open the temple doors. As always, they creaked loudly. She remembered how, when Ruler was alive, she had told them to oil it.

Swim Swim ducked into a Nishimonzen alley. No moon was out. Compared to other areas, Nishimonzen had barely any streetlamps, some residents complained. But the local government never responded to the complaints, so the alley was dark. She couldn't sense anyone following her. Ruler had always said, "You're all free to do as you please" when she got fed up with them, but the angels and Tama seemed to be obeying.

She had idolized Ruler. When she'd suddenly become a magical girl and had no idea what to do, it was Ruler who had come and taught her. She'd reminded her of the princesses in her dreams, and Swim Swim loyally carried out her teachings.

"Your leader must be the object of your affection. The organization is most effective when everyone tries to imitate her."

And so Swim Swim obeyed. Her mentor was a princess, and princesses were always right. She was strong, clever, lovely, and overflowing with leadership. Swim Swim tried to be like her, but

Ruler herself was the biggest thing in the way of that goal. Two rulers meant that neither was truly in charge, because a ruler stood above all. Swim Swim adored and revered Ruler, but in order for her to take the final step, her leader had to die. The night she realized this, Swim Swim threw up everything she'd eaten that day and broke into a fever. She'd skipped two days of school. But it had to be done. Swim Swim wanted to be like Ruler more than anything.

But Ruler's magic was powerful. Swim Swim would have to work hard to take her out. She knew the Peaky Angels and Tama were unhappy with Ruler, but even with their help, she would still have to deal with the leader's orders. She decided to wait for the right opportunity.

It wasn't long before that chance presented itself: the plot to steal Snow White's magical candy. Of Snow White's nearly 50,000 pieces of candy, she took 37,000, grabbed the dazed Tama underneath the steel tower and forced 35,000 onto her, and reported to Ruler that there had only been 2,000 pieces. The 35,000 pieces she'd given to Tama she split evenly between all the magical girls except for Ruler, Snow White, and La Pucelle. Some were suspicious, some were on guard, some were openly hostile, and some fired before asking questions. Nobody welcomed them, even though they were there to share their candy, but nobody turned it down.

She'd used Fav to contact the others. His connection with everyone allowed him to contact any magical girl, even if they tried to hide where they were. Fav was short-spoken and tended to not explain well, but he tried to help as much as he could when they asked. Swim Swim had learned this from Ruler, too.

Divided among eleven people, the 35,000 pieces gave them 3,180 each. She'd left Snow White with more than 10,000 pieces, meaning if she split evenly with La Pucelle, they'd each have 5,000. And so Ruler, convinced that her 1,044 pieces meant she couldn't possibly get the ax, ended up with the lowest amount of candy.

The Peaky Angels had enthusiastically agreed to the plan, and Tama, though clearly a little guilty, also agreed. They accepted Swim Swim as their leader.

She had succeeded in taking out Ruler without giving her a chance to use her magic or even realize she'd been betrayed.

She laid the body at the end of the main street. It was light to carry, even for someone without magical strength, and long gone cold.

"Good-bye, and thank you for everything."

Swim Swim bowed deeply, turned her back on Ruler's corpse, and disappeared into the darkness of the alley. Ruler was gone, but she'd left behind her many teachings. No matter what the future held, she'd stay true to them. Wiping a tear with her fingertip, Swim Swim ran off into the gloom.

CHAPTER 3
THE MAGICAL KNIGHT

As the days went by, the leaves on the evenly spaced gingko trees lining the main street turned from green to yellow, completing their transformation. It felt like just yesterday that the sun was high even during evening, which made the rust-red sky seem lonely and almost colder than a normal winter's day.

Shizuku Ashu drew the curtains closed and spoke to the room.

"People look so small from a sixth-floor apartment. The smaller they look, the less human they seem."

"You think so too, Shizuku?"

"I suppose it's not very magical girl–esque of me to say."

"But it's certainly Shizuku-esque of you to puzzle over ideas."

Nana Habutae chuckled, and Shizuku's expression softened. It seemed like ages since she'd last smiled. Whether as Nana Habutae or as Sister Nana, she only wore sadness and tears lately, never smiles.

The apartment was in Nana's name, but Shizuku was practically her roommate. She came and went freely, returning to her own place barely even once a week.

Shizuku had been popular in middle and high school. Ever since childhood, she had received compliments for her face, fair as an angel's or an elf's, and becoming Winterprison didn't change her outer appearance much. She was most certainly a girl, but the androgynous and mysterious air around her made her popular with about 30 percent boys and 70 percent girls. She had experience with both, having dated both sexes, but none of those relationships ever lasted very long. However, her relationship with Nana had lasted, uncharacteristically so.

The two first met in a university seminar. Eventually they became friends, spending weekends together, and Nana showed Shizuku the game she'd been playing recently, *Magical Girl Raising Project*. Thus, it seemed like fate that when she was chosen, Nana was, too. However, that wasn't the reason they remained together. Shizuku wasn't a doe-eyed young girl, enamored with "soul mates" and the like—she'd been drawn to Nana since before her transformation.

"I guess her smile's just too cute."

"Did you say something?"

"No, just muttering to myself."

She sat on the sofa, crossed her legs, and rested her weight on the armrest. Nana constantly insisted it was unsightly, that it could hardly be comfortable, and that it looked like a monk's self-flagellation, but this position was most relaxing to Shizuku. She could only be like this when she was in a safe place, free of the danger of being attacked.

The bookshelf was packed with romance novels, manga, and collections of romantic poems, and the light pink wallpaper, upon close inspection, bore a faint heart pattern. Pinned to a corkboard were pictures of Sister Nana and Winterprison, aka Nana Habutae and Shizuku Ashu, smiling. One in particular drew Shizuku's eye, and she stood up. One of its corners was bent, so she flattened it out and made sure it was straight, then returned to the couch.

"You're such a perfectionist."

"Some would just call it fussy."

"So you're aware, then?" Nana laughed again. "Don't make me laugh while I'm dealing with fire."

"Is today's menu curry?"

"Close, but no cigar."

"Then is it stew?"

"That's right, a spikenard cream stew. It'll take a while to remove the bitterness, so be patient, okay?"

Shizuku's expression clouded, in stark contrast to Nana's as she lightly stirred the pot with a ladle. *Spikenard? Cream stew? It's not even the season for them...*

Nana was constantly worrying about the fact that she was heavier than normal. Because of this, she refused to eat what she would have liked to in the name of her diet.

"You don't need to suffer to get skinny. Besides, your roundness is healthy and, more importantly, cute." The one time Shizuku had tried to give her heartfelt advice, Nana had ignored her for three days. *You're skinny when you transform into a magical girl, so what's the problem?* she thought to herself, but made sure to never say it out loud. She could never understand Nana's maiden heart, but she had to pretend to or she would get the cold shoulder again.

Lately Nana had not only restrained her appetite, but tried to limit herself to vegetables. Somehow she procured mountain vegetables for dishes Shizuku had never heard of. Of course, alien dishes meant alien flavors, and each new one puzzled Shizuku.

Still...

It's just good to see her smiling, she thought.

Nana was normally a cheerful girl, and she had glowed with joy over being able to save others as a classic heroine. But ever since the number of active magical girls within the city had hit sixteen and they had been forced to fight one another, that glow had faded.

Shizuku—Winterprison—knew what she had to do.

Nemurin. Ruler. So far there had been two. Only six remained to be cut. She had to make sure Sister Nana did not end up one of them. Just imagining her death broke Shizuku's heart.

Something hadn't seemed right about Ruler's demise, and Swim Swim's offer of a massive amount of points for free was definitely related. Some among them weren't content to simply gather candy like the rules stated.

She picked up the glass fish decoration on the table and peered through it at Nana working in the kitchen. The distorted figure of the other girl appeared much slimmer. A smile crept onto her face, so to disguise it she called out to Nana.

"Let's go out after we eat. You have any plans today?"

"I was thinking of going to Mount Takanami."

"I don't approve of you going out too far. It's dangerous right now."

"I'll be fine with you around. But I really must go today."

"Why?"

"The Musician of the Forest, Cranberry, contacted me and insisted we meet. Maybe she's heard about our efforts. Maybe this time she'll agree to help…"

Nana smiled weakly. She was probably stressed because Top Speed hadn't reacted favorably and Ripple was pretty much hostile. Shizuku just wanted to give her a hug.

The meeting was at two in the morning, in a quarry at Mount Takanami.

The Musician of the Forest, Cranberry—Nana had seen her in chat before, but had never met her in real life. She had only "seen" her and not "talked with" her because, though Cranberry had a high chat attendance rate, she hardly ever said anything. All she did was serenade them with background music. She was a mysterious one. Didn't everyone who attended the chat—except for Winterprison, who was only there to accompany another—do so because they wanted to talk? But despite the fact that she attended every chat, she remained silent and never interjected.

Sister Nana was excited for a potential new comrade, but Winterprison was on her guard. Sometimes the ones with no obvious goals or principles were more trouble than those who were openly dangerous.

Cranberry arrived right on time.

"Good evening, Sister Nana. Weiss Winterprison."

"Good evening, Musician of the Forest, Cranberry."

"Just Cranberry is fine, Sister Nana."

"Very well, Cranberry. I've seen you many times in chat, but this is our first time meeting in person."

"You two are just as I imagined. I'm a little surprised."

While Winterprison simply lowered her head slightly and gave a curt "Thanks," the other two conversed merrily and easily. In chat, Cranberry was stubbornly taciturn, but actually talking to her, she seemed like a modest adult woman fluent in societal niceties.

Long, pointed ears poked out from beneath her casually flowing blond hair, while thin vines dotted with flowers of all sizes wrapped around her shoulders, feet, waist, and thighs. She wore a frilled blouse and grass green jacket held together by an amber pin, and the top half of her outfit seemed quite modest. But downstairs, her thighs were almost completely exposed, and this, combined with her twenty-year-old appearance—ancient for a magical girl—made it all the more stimulating. After listening to Sister Nana's passionate proposal, she slowly opened her mouth.

"I have a question for you, if that's all right?"

"Yes, please. We'll answer anything we can."

"Could you stop this?"

"Huh?"

"Stop trying to spoil the game."

Sister Nana turned to Winterprison for help. She seemed absolutely baffled. Winterprison removed her right hand from the pocket she'd stuck it in, and a smile crept onto Cranberry's face.

"Err... What is the meaning of that?"

"Exactly what you think it means."

Winterprison took a step forward in front of the confused Sister Nana, shielding her.

"Winterprison. I've wanted to fight you since the day I heard the rumors."

"What?"

"That no one's ever successfully made you use your right arm in hand-to-hand combat."

Winterprison quickly took note of her surroundings: to the right, a cliff; to the left, piles of gravel; below her, stones scattered about. The weather was fairly clear, and she could see no traps or ambushes prepared. The quarry was more accurately an abandoned quarry, as the construction company that owned the land had disbanded long ago. Everything valuable, from machines to supplies, had already been seized and dismantled, the useless junk left among the stones of various shapes and sizes. Cranberry's courteous behavior remained unaffected. Her aura hadn't changed, either.

Slowly, she took a step forward.

She was in range. The moment Winterprison realized this, Cranberry unleashed a lightning-fast high kick. Winterprison managed to block with her left arm, but the blow was heavy, and her bones creaked. The tremendous force tousled her scarf. With a small yelp, Sister Nana fell onto her butt.

"That long scarf suits this quarry quite nicely."

Cranberry's fingers shot toward her opponent's face, causing Winterprison to use her magic—wall creation. The material of the walls changed depending on where she was, so in a quarry it was stone. Standing six feet high, three feet wide, and an inch thick, the monolith split the ground between them. Cranberry's assault, however, pierced through it easily and turned it to rubble, forcing Winterprison to roll on the ground to dodge.

Cranberry was stronger physically than the average magical girl, but she didn't simply attack. She used martial arts. Beneath her movements flowed the confidence of a veteran. Without hesitation she had struck at the eye—and the brain right behind it. She was clearly aiming to kill.

"Winterprison!"

"Get back, Sister Nana."

She needed to widen the gap between them and get Sister Nana away from the enemy. With those two goals in mind, Winterprison retreated a step. The quarry was littered with obstacles, forcing her to pay attention for even simple movements, but Cranberry didn't seem to watch her step at all as she approached. She took no offensive stance. She simply smiled.

She demolished, obliterated, and even scaled wall after wall. As barriers, Winterprison's stone defenses were utterly useless, couldn't even slow her down. They weren't weak, either, because they were reinforced with magic. Stone or not, they should have been stronger than steel, but before Cranberry's unnatural strength they were no better than wood fences.

Predicting an attack, Winterprison took another half step back. But the attack she expected never came. Cranberry stepped forward, closing the vast gap. Winterprison blocked the low kick with her shin and felt a dull pain—her attacker's pointed toes drove straight into her.

From low, Cranberry went high. The arc of her kick aimed at Winterprison's head turned, slipped through her guard, and found purchase in her rib cage. The blow was powerful enough to knock the air out of her lungs.

And she didn't stop. From middle to high, Cranberry's toes struck at Winterprison's temple. Staggered as she was, Winterprison couldn't fully avoid the attack. It sliced her cheek open, sent blood and flesh flying, broke her cheekbone, shattered her teeth. She could hear the damage directly in her eardrums. Slamming her foot down, Winterprison barely stayed standing.

Then she felt a new energy in the pit of her stomach. It was magic. Not her original power, though—Sister Nana was giving her strength. Now she could fight back.

By the time Winterprison was internally ready to counterattack, Cranberry's leg was already in front of her face. She tightly wound her scarf around it before the other girl could react. While symbolic, the garment was no mere decoration. It was a weapon. Like lightning, she yanked back with all her weight to snag Cranberry's leg. Focusing entirely on her hands, gripping hard enough to break bone, she swung up and then down, and

Cranberry hurtled toward a wall she'd just created. Unable to break the fall, her head crashed against the stone and sprayed blood everywhere.

The girl's body bounced and rolled along the gravel, and Winterprison gave chase. She flung up a barricade to cut off any escape route and stop her in her tracks, then grabbed her. She tumbled with her in a tangle of limbs, clutched Cranberry by the arms, pinned her legs, pulled her long hair, and finally tied her up with it. Straddling Cranberry, Winterprison glared down at her.

She hit her without mercy. Once, twice, three, four, five, six, seven times. Cranberry seemed to be rolling with the punches in an effort to reduce the damage. Winterprison continued the onslaught. There was no need to finish it with one blow. Little by little, they would add up. Over and over, until she could hear the pain.

"Winterprison! Behind you!" she heard Sister Nana cry out. She whirled around, but there was nothing there—only Sister Nana, looking dumbfounded. A heavy blow struck the back of her head and sent her flying from her seat on top of Cranberry. Winterprison grasped at the gravel with her fingertips to slow herself, then balled her hand into a fist as she kneeled.

She'd reacted instinctively to Sister Nana's voice behind her, but there had been nothing. All she'd done was give Cranberry a giant opening. There was no way Sister Nana had tried to distract her on purpose, and her confusion suggested she hadn't even done the screaming in the first place.

Cranberry's magic, then?

Within her blurry vision, she could see Cranberry trying to stand. Winterprison activated her magic as she stood, then rocketed toward her. Though it would seem counterintuitive, she placed the wall between her and Cranberry. It would be destroyed without any real effort, so she just needed to block off the enemy's sight for a moment.

Winterprison picked up Sister Nana, leaped toward the cliff opposite Cranberry, and retreated from the quarry.

◇◇◇

They'd gotten away.

Cranberry knew Mount Takanami like the back of her hand. Not to mention her five senses, especially her hearing, far exceeded mortal limits. She was confident she could catch them if she pursued.

But she didn't. She gazed down from atop the cliff, saw that the shrubbery and incline blocked off most of the view, and shrugged.

"You're letting them get away, pon?"

The voice from her magical phone was vaguely scornful and accusing. Cranberry was impressed that a synthetic voice could pull off such a skillful imitation.

"Didn't you say you were going to finish off Sister Nana, pon? Letting her live won't help the game progress, pon."

"That...may not be entirely true."

How long had it been since Cranberry last fought someone on equal ground like that? How long since someone had made her use her magic?

Her powers allowed her to control sound. Her "Winterprison! Behind you!" in Sister Nana's voice had distracted her opponent long enough for a strike to the defenseless back of her head. If Cranberry hadn't been restrained, she could have killed her, but instead Winterprison had escaped merely wounded.

Weiss Winterprison was stronger than anyone she'd ever fought. She'd gone toe-to-toe with Cranberry, albeit with the help of Sister Nana. Faced with an opponent she could finally go all-out on, joy bubbled up within her, like a light sparkling deep inside her brain. The experience made her feel like a girl in love. Perhaps she was.

For a proper fight with her, Cranberry would need to get rid of her source of restraint, Sister Nana. Yet without her, Winterprison wasn't all that strong. It was unfortunate all around, really.

"I want time to think. Let's just put things on hold for now."

"How irresponsible, pon."

"Then what about this? I'll search for anyone sympathetic to Sister Nana…and eliminate the strongest ones."

The biggest requirement was that they be strong. Fighting to kill, lives on the line—only then was she not alone. Blood flowing, flesh flying, entrails spilling, each understanding the other perfectly. The only restriction was that her opponent must be strong. She didn't want to break the communication with a single attack.

She was aware that her thirst for battle was bordering on suicidal, but she would never have accepted this role if there was no fighting involved. Cranberry had no plans to change herself. Blood poured from her nose without stopping as the battle-crazed Musician of the Forest wiped it with her wrist.

Swim Swim, in her new position as leader, inherited Ruler's will on a basic level, but also made it her own. She knew that was what Ruler would have done in her shoes. She still prioritized stealing candy over earning it herself, but now she was wiser about her methods. In attacking Snow White, they had challenged her head-on and barely succeeded. La Pucelle had been stronger than expected, and her ability to fight off three of them and come to Snow White's aid was the reason their success was so narrow. If Snow White had been as strong as La Pucelle, if La Pucelle had been any stronger, if either had possessed some incredible magic—then the plan would have certainly ended in empty failure.

But that was what happened when you attacked head-on. Why not attack from the side, or the back? Swim Swim considered all her options. What could she do? What should she do? How could she best gain the most candy? How should she disable her opponent and take theirs? Over and over and over she thought, until the Peaky Angels made a suggestion.

"How about we sabotage the person in first place?" "A smear campaign, huh? Sis, you're so magi-cool."

And so they took to the message boards and started perpetrating terrible rumors about Snow White. It was surreal to see the twin angels sitting in the corner of the temple, their heads huddled together as they typed away on magical phones.

"I'll say that girl in white mugged me!" "Then I'll say the witch screamed at me!" "And the ninja kicked me!" "The nun punched my shoulder!"

Swim Swim started to wonder if Ruler would have found a better method after all.

"Thank you for the food."

After finishing dinner, Koyuki put down her bowl and sighed. She could feel someone watching her, and when she raised her head, she discovered it was her father. His worry and curiosity were unmistakable. Koyuki shifted uncomfortably in her seat.

"Wh-what?"

"Oh… Nothing."

For some reason, he hesitated and slapped his forehead below a receding hairline. He was acting odd. Normally, the patriarch of the Himekawa household expressed himself more clearly. The sounds of her mother doing the dishes in the kitchen were the same as always.

"Seriously, what, Dad? You're weirding me out."

"You've just seemed down lately."

Koyuki reacted with shock, and she stared at her father in his pajamas. Everything but his hair was startlingly similar to how it was years ago. The more she grew, the more people commented that she resembled him, but she couldn't for the life of her see how.

"You're eating less, too. You barely moved your chopsticks yesterday. You're pale. Mom thinks it might be boy troubles."

From the kitchen came a loud shout, "I told you not to say that!"

"Today…you seemed more down than usual, but you at least ate all your food. That's a relief."

"Uh, right."

"I guess that means you found some answers, then."

"Yeah, I guess."

"So, was it a boy?"

"Dad! God!"

She stood up and nearly tripped as she ran down the hall and up the stairs, and then she collapsed on her bed.

So they knew she was depressed. In other words, she'd caused them a lot of worry. She'd felt guilty, but the comment about boys made her forget that instantly. For a second, Souta's face popped into her head, then changed to La Pucelle. Koyuki shook her head to dispel the image.

School, work, and earning magical candies. At school, she worked toward her future; at her job, she worked to preserve her present; and when she was a magical girl, she worked to keep herself alive. She couldn't slack off on any of it. The only times Kano could think were before bed, in the bath, and on the way home from school.

The walk from her place to the station was five minutes, and the walk from her school to the station was seven minutes. For the thirty-five minutes between stations, including transfers, Kano rocked with the motion of the trains. Back when she'd had money she'd bought a train pass, but it would only last until the end of the third trimester of her second year. In her third year, she'd have to buy a bicycle, and if she couldn't find one for cheap, she'd be forced to walk to school. So she decided she would at least get the most out of the peaceful train commute while she still could.

To and from school, her train was always full of middle schoolers. Kano stood alone amid the schoolmates and their idle chitchat, staring out the window. Among the sights was a big red diamond signboard for Koushu Chinese restaurant. It was famous for its delicious boiled dumplings, but crows tended to swarm in the trash area behind the restaurant. The owner was also famously stubborn, so complaints about this went unheard. Perhaps she could do something.

The building in front of the station was a municipal parking garage ready to collapse at any moment. The very first step of the stairway between the first and second floors was rusted and pocked with small holes. The place was badly in need of repair. Someone would get hurt sooner or later. Unfortunately, any reports would most likely fall on deaf ears. Perhaps she should ask Top Speed if she owned any repair tools.

Directly next to a supermarket and its bright signs was a pedestrian bridge. About once every three days, at around ten PM, a broad-shouldered, middle-aged man would sit on the bench there, which made her quite curious. From his dress he seemed to have a steady job, but he always hung his head with pain on his face. Perhaps she should talk to him one day.

These thoughts ran through her head like the train running through Nakayado. Kano retrieved her phone from her school bag—not her magical one, but her regular phone. The Internet was still buzzing with magical-girl sightings. And of course, Snow White's surpassed everyone else's. Whenever she thought of Nakayado, Kano wondered if she just wanted to earn candy, or if she simply cared that deeply for her assigned area. Two months ago, it would have definitely been the former. Now she wasn't so sure. The former seemed more like Kano, while the latter seemed, like the motivation of an irritating busybody. Still, she couldn't say.

Kano's desperate need for candy had led her to investigate every bit of Nakayado. As a result, from the trash situation of a Chinese restaurant to the stairs of a parking garage, there was nothing Kano didn't know. Once, she'd shown Top Speed just the tip of her vast knowledge, and the other girl had praised her, saying, "Wow, you know everything! That's the kinda love a magical girl should have for her neighborhood!" Kano had simply clicked her tongue over the big fuss, but she wasn't exactly unhappy about it.

Did Snow White also think about such things while helping

people? Kano read further down the page. There were stories of how the girl in white helped fix a bike chain, not caring that her dress would get stained, and how once she'd comforted a crying child, even though she looked like she wanted to cry herself. It was all rumors, but the actions and behavior painted a vivid picture of her true character.

Hearing the announcement for her station, Kano returned her phone to her bag.

Winterprison took her near-loss quite hard. And the attack from someone who'd agreed to a discussion had wounded Sister Nana. Bitterness filled Winterprison over losing at her specialty, hand-to-hand combat, even if she had been distracted by magic. Her inability to protect Sister Nana had been traumatic, but that was nothing compared to how Sister Nana herself must have felt. Her overconfidence had led her to hurt and not kill her opponent, but she swore that the next time they met she'd kill that piece of trash with one blow.

But for the battered Sister Nana, there was no time to rest.

The day after their battle with Cranberry, she learned she would be mentoring the newest addition to their ranks. Winterprison urged her to cancel or ask for more time, but the haggard Sister Nana stubbornly refused to do either.

Magical girls healed quickly, so Winterprison's wounds were already completely gone. Sister Nana's heart, however, showed no signs of mending. As she tottered forward, Winterprison followed two steps behind, thinking, *If this newbie tries to harm Sister Nana, there will be no mercy.*

A deep, dark night covered the town of Kobiki. The impenetrable gloom hid even the presences of magical girls. There were no tall buildings, but away from the lampposts no one could spot a few people having a conversation. Taking advantage of this,

Winterprison and Sister Nana chose to have the meeting in front of an abandoned factory.

The area, long ago nicknamed Lumber Street, had suffered an extended period of recession that caused many businesses to close their doors and shut down their factories. Only reckless idiots looking to test their courage, professional thieves, and weirdos lurked here anymore. Most likely, a magical girl would be considered a weirdo rather than a thief, Winterprison thought disparagingly. But at that moment, Sister Nana entered her line of sight and quickly banished the thought.

Sister Nana was a saint, willing to sacrifice herself to save another. Winterprison didn't consider herself even close to a saint, but she would die for the other woman's sake.

But what about the other one in front of her?

With her basically normal clothes, Winterprison didn't have much room to judge, but this girl's outfit was relatively plain. She seemed almost like the main character from one of the books on Nana Habutae's bookshelf—*Alice's Adventures in Wonderland*, come to life—except for the color. In the book, the main character didn't wear all black. This Alice, black as a wet crow's feather from head to toe, and silent as a mouse, resembled someone returning from a funeral in their mourning clothes. In her right arm, she held a white rabbit that, rather than looking cute, reinforced her creepiness.

Her clothes weren't the only element of her unhealthy image, though. Magical girls, even outlaws like Calamity Mary or crazies like Cranberry, had beautiful skin, smooth cheeks, and healthy proportions. They showed their physical beauty in its natural form.

But this person—Hardgore Alice, the newbie under Sister Nana's mentorship—had deep bags under her dead, black eyes. She stood slightly hunched, her pale lips parted about a pinkie's width, her arms dangling limply at each side. Her complexion was more pale than white, like a person with constant indigestion.

It was impossible to tell if she was truly listening as Sister Nana

prattled on passionately despite her depression. To Winterprison, it seemed like she was spacing out.

"Now is the time to band together. We have to pool our knowledge and think together to avoid any more victims. We need an idea to break out of our present dilemma."

No answer. Not a sign that she was listening. She probably hadn't even blinked. Hardgore Alice hadn't moved a muscle since introducing herself.

The whole reason they were in this predicament in the first place was because a sixteenth magical girl had been added. So shouldn't Alice, as the sixteenth, feel a little guilty? If she wasn't planning on listening, the least she could do was pretend. Sister Nana deserved that much.

Alice annoyed Winterprison, and the frustration only burned hotter as time went on.

Sister Nana explained that the purpose of magic was to make others happy. No response.

She shared her experience of Calamity Mary's attack. No response.

She explained how they earned candy by performing good deeds, and that once a week the girl with the lowest amount of candy was cut from the roster. No response.

She recounted her regret over Nemurin. No response.

A little perplexed, she shared how Ruler had been cut. No response.

Even their tussle with the crazy Cranberry. No response.

Winterprison was approaching the limit of her patience. From her cool appearance and quiet demeanor, most would say she was calm and logical, but in actuality Winterprison had a short temper. She was just about ready to yell at the girl.

"I heard that Snow White was attacked the other day. I bet they were after her candy. She's been the undisputed top candy earner, after all. Oh, despicable…"

Alice's shoulder twitched.

"This Snow White."

Sister Nana stopped talking. She'd nearly missed the small whisper—the first time Alice had opened her mouth since they'd met.

"Is that the white magical girl?"

"Huh?"

"Is Snow White the white magical girl?"

"Yes, that's right."

"And her clothes are like a school uniform?"

"Yes."

"Do you know where she is?"

"I believe she was designated Kubegahama. Isn't that right?" The last bit was directed at Winterprison, but before she could respond, Alice turned on her heel and ran off. Her footsteps faded into the distance.

"Does she even know how to say thank you?" she muttered, fully aware it was beside the point.

"Do you think…she went to go help Snow White?"

Winterprison found it more likely that she'd excitedly rushed off to steal from the girl with the most candy, but she knew the idea would upset Sister Nana, so she nodded stonily.

La Pucelle was sorry. Deeply, deeply sorry. Deeply, deeply, deeply, deeply, deeply sorry. She was sorry she'd been so naive as to think the update to the magical phones would only be used for willing transfers. She should have foreseen that people would use it to steal. That way, she would have been more on guard.

She was sorry for making the steel tower in Kubegahama her meeting place with Snow White. They'd even talked about it in chat, so it was practically public knowledge. That was probably the most appealing point for any potential criminals looking to attack.

She was sorry for being so sure she and Snow White shared the same ideals. Snow White had never wanted to fight. Arrogance had made La Pucelle believe their vision of what a magical girl should be was the same.

She was sorry for not realizing the initial attack was a diversion until it was actually said out loud. She'd been so excited at the chance to use her full power, drunk on it, that she had put Snow White in danger. It was completely her fault that 37,000 pieces of candy had been stolen.

But she wasn't just sorry. La Pucelle actively worked to make sure everything she did as a magical girl went safer and smoother than ever before. Every day they changed their meeting spot. To minimize risk, they split their candy between them. Whenever they were together, they'd talk with their backs to each other. This way, they could respond to attacks from either side.

Then there was the shame.

She'd sworn to protect Snow White no matter what, yet only a few days later they'd been utterly defeated. It was unbearable. She was so ashamed she couldn't bring herself to look at her friend. Yet, of course, she couldn't afford not to. There was no telling when something similar might happen again, and that was when she would need to protect her. Snow White, however, had become depressed despite being saved. La Pucelle desperately wanted to cheer her up.

Seeing Snow White's sadness upset her. The fact that someone had stolen her candy—that a magical girl would think to steal another's candy—had shocked her. La Pucelle's attempts at conversation mostly received half-hearted replies. If she said nothing, the only sound between them would be the night wind blowing as they both stared off into the distance.

She remembered how, as a child, Snow White—Koyuki Himekawa—had hated fighting. She was the kind of girl who cried over fights that didn't involve her in the slightest. Of all the magical girls, she was the least suited to stealing and hurting others.

La Pucelle had to protect her.

The memory of Snow White in her arms atop the steel tower made her heart race. Her blood ran cold as she remembered the attack.

Now Snow White was no longer by her side. She'd already gone home.

"Good evening."

"Hey."

Suddenly, a voice came from behind, but La Pucelle answered without shock or panic. She'd felt the presence all night. Something had been observing them, and while she'd sensed it, Snow White had seemed unaware.

"Seems you noticed me."

"Yeah."

"Of course. But then why did you let Snow White leave?"

"Because this'll be easier alone."

"Well, well… That makes this simpler."

The seventh port warehouse was shorter than the steel tower, but it was closer to the ocean, so the thick, salty scent of the waves on the wind was stronger. From the gaps between the clouds, stars flickered in and out of view. The one facing La Pucelle appeared quite old. All the magical girls she knew, enemy or friend, looked to be between ten and nineteen, but this one was at least twenty.

"La Pucelle, I heard you were victorious in a three-on-one battle."

"I wouldn't really call it a victory."

"No need to be modest. It's better for me if it's the truth. Your strength is the only reason I would challenge you."

La Pucelle blinked.

"You're not after my candy?"

"I am the Musician of the Forest, Cranberry. I have no need for candy. All I want is a strong opponent."

A magical girl who's not trying to steal candy, eh? It had only been a few days since the last attack, so being on her guard wasn't unwarranted. She was a bit embarrassed she'd been so quick to judge, though. To hide her embarrassment, she smacked the roof of the warehouse with her tail.

Still, this girl was crazy to stalk strong opponents to battle. Well, if she wanted a fight, La Pucelle would give one to her. She liked these sorts of situations. Two people aiming to be the strongest would meet each other and have a clean, fair fight, acknowledging each other's power. She'd seen it so many times in manga and anime and had always dreamed of something similar.

"My name is La Pucelle. Musician of the Forest, Cranberry, I accept your challenge."

"Thank you very much."

La Pucelle drew her sword, and Cranberry readied her fists. The salt spray licked at the two combatants as they squared off atop the warehouse, rustling the flowers decorating Cranberry's body. The blossoms reminded La Pucelle of Snow White, but Cranberry's were darker, fresher, and more vibrant.

CHAT #3

Fav: Well, time for another exciting chat, pon!

Fav: Uh…but no one seems to be here, pon

Fav: Three weeks in and we're down to two. That's kind of a problem, pon

Fav: Well, no matter, pon. Everyone looks at the logs anyway

Fav: Cranberry, thank you for always attending, pon

Fav: No one else is here, so it's fine if you play your music

Fav: Well, there are three announcements today, pon

Fav: Two pieces of good news, and one piece of bad news

Fav: Let's go with the good news first, pon

Fav: The magical phones have received another update, pon

Fav: You can now download useful items, pon

Fav: There are five in total!

Fav: They're all on a first-come, first-served basis, so remember, the early bird gets the worm, pon!

Fav: Now for the bad news, pon

Fav: La Pucelle has died in an accident, pon. This is very sad, pon. Heartbreaking, pon

Fav: But everyone, do your best not to let this sacrifice be in vain, pon

Fav: And the last piece of good news:

Fav: Because La Pucelle is dead, no one is getting cut this week

Fav: So, see you next week!
Fav: Oh, and the top earner hates having her results announced, so that is canceled, pon
Fav: Thank you for your understanding

The music from the magical phone no longer reached her ears. At home, at school, even at the funeral, Snow White had held it in, but now she screamed into the howling winds—she writhed, wailed, and punched the steel tower. Unable to consider why it had happened or what this meant for her, Snow White cried. She sobbed and grieved over the death of La Pucelle—Souta Kishibe.

CHAPTER 4
THE MOONLIT MAGICAL GIRL

La Pucelle's death meant no one was cut that week. No one really questioned the cause of death, either. *If someone dies, I'm not cut. If I kill someone, I'm not cut. If I want to live, I should kill.* That was the best mind-set, and eventually everyone would come to realize that.

"You think it'll be that easy?"

"It will, it will. The medium to gather people this time is a mobile game aimed at a younger demographic, pon. That's drawn in lots of them, and they're all young. Their youth makes them particularly emotional, so all we need to do is add a little fuel to the fire, pon."

Fav was the one who had suggested using a mobile game as the medium. Meaning he probably wanted to claim the success as his own. Cranberry had first met Fav some time ago, but this part of him still rubbed her the wrong way. Most likely, Fav also found Cranberry to be a pain as well. That was how work relationships should be.

Cranberry rolled onto the bed and tapped her magical phone. A new header had been added to the start screen for *Magical Girl Raising Project*, entitled GET ITEMS.

Four-Dimensional Bag: Can hold items of any size or weight that can be carried by one person. Its fourth dimension gives it unlimited storage.

Invisibility Cloak: Makes the wearer invisible to others. Also erases smell, so dogs can't find you.

Weapon: A weapon you can add to your costume. Can stand up to the abuse of superpowered combat. You may choose your weapon from the list. Give it a cool name!

Energy Pills: Medicine that makes you really pumped! This doesn't heal wounds, so don't make that mistake. Some side effects may occur from overuse. Ten pills per container.

Rabbit's Foot: Brings good luck when you're in big trouble. Whether that saves you or not still depends on you, so don't rely on it too much.

In total, there were five downloadable items, and all of them were everyday tools from the Magical Kingdom. However, they each came with a price in order to use them. Fav, of course, had proudly announced that these items with irreversible effects would up the intensity of the fighting and cut off any means of escape for the girls.

Cranberry spoke into the device.

"Fav."

"Yes, yes, master? What is your request, pon?"

The black-and-white sphere with butterfly wings faded in from a corner of the screen.

"Are you sure adding these items won't ruin our goal of cultivating the strong? Some of these might allow the weaker ones to overcome the stronger ones."

"If that's all it takes to kill them, then they weren't really that strong to begin with, pon."

Fav did a flip in the air, scattering scales.

"Magical girls aren't just users of magic, pon. The ones who pass that shallow selection test from the Magical Kingdom aren't true magical girls at all, pon. They must be heroines, pon. If they die some silly death just because items were added to the game, they're failures. Just consider them side characters that were supposed to die, pon."

Inside the screen, Fav's mouth twisted ever so slightly into what looked like a truly ominous smile.

"Hey, master! Fighting tough opponents is enough for you, right? And you hate a selection test that doesn't choose the strongest survivors, right? So this is just fine! This sets up the true magical girls to brutally crush the ones who scheme and suck up to survive."

After finishing his spiel, Fav did another flip and returned to his usual expressionless demeanor.

"That's about it, pon."

"I see."

"Fav is trying to grant your wish to fight at full power, so the least you can do is grant Fav's wish for a super intense spectacle, pon. That's our contract, pon."

"Am I part of this spectacle as well?"

"Maybe."

Fav smiled, his expression unchanging.

"Are these items…free?"

"*Magical Girl Raising Project* is always free to play. You will never be charged money, pon."

"But there are numbers under the names. The bag has a ten, the cloak has a twenty-five, the weapon's five, the medicine's three, the rabbit's foot's six…"

"You won't pay money, but Fav never said there wouldn't be a price, pon."

"So I do have to pay something?"

"Part of your life, pon. The weapon takes five years, the bag ten. The cloak takes twenty-five years. The stronger a magical item, the greater the price you have to pay to create it. But for girls like you with magic that isn't suited for fighting, this is a bailout, pon. You're supposed to use these items to close the gap between you and the others, pon. When things are this dangerous, what's a bit of your life that you don't even know you have?"

Snow White leaned against the concrete-block wall and slid down. Maybe it was the dirty alley, devoid of even drunkards and stray dogs, but she felt alone in the world. She'd sought out a place to spend some time by herself, but the solitude was torture. She wiped her sticky, sweaty cheek with the back of her hand. Her skin was pale as a ghost's, too.

Souta Kishibe's death had been explained as a traffic accident. Snow White had attended the wake and funeral as Koyuki Himekawa, but she couldn't bring herself to look at his corpse because it was so mutilated. The car that hit him had been discovered in a parking garage, but it was a stolen vehicle. The police still hadn't found the driver.

Snow White wiped her eyes. This time, her hand was covered in tears. She'd thought they all dried up after she sobbed her eyes out over La Pucelle's death, but just remembering her friend made them well and overflow again.

"Sou..."

She remembered the first day they'd talked atop the steel tower. The day she saved her from the candy thieves. The day she swore to be the sword that protected her. The day they shared their magic with each other and pinkie promised to not tell the others. The day she risked her life to save a kid from an oncoming car and later said, embarrassedly, "My body just moved on its own." The day they celebrated a web post that called her a knight who protected a child. The days of discourse over manga and anime. The days they sat together and watched anime as children.

She recalled how, as Souta, he had looked at her with such jealousy when she proclaimed she'd become a magical girl. How, as

La Pucelle, she had proudly shown her that a boy could become a magical girl after all. How, as Souta, he walked to school kicking a soccer ball. How Souta's mom bawled over losing her son who had just entered middle school...

His warmth as he held her. The heat blooming deep in her chest.

Time seemed to blur. Memory after memory floated through her mind and disappeared. She couldn't go on like this. It wasn't right. She knew this, but her heart was frozen in place. It wouldn't let her move forward.

"Sou... Sou..."

"Cry all you like. No one's going to pity you, pon."

Her magical phone had fallen screen-side down, which muffled Fav's voice more than usual. It sounded as if the creature was somewhere else.

"Do you think if you snivel and whine, someone will come save you, pon? Are you going to let La Pucelle's sacrifice go to waste, pon?"

The word *sacrifice* weighed on her back like a cross. They still hadn't captured the driver that ran over Souta. Was his killer actually a human, though? She knew it was a horrifying thing to consider, but she couldn't get it out of her mind.

Could one of her fellows have killed Souta? Was there a magical girl in the city capable of killing others like her? If so, then if she got one of those new items...

"Cheer up—for La Pucelle's sake, too, pon. Summon some courage and choose an item, pon."

Snow White shakily reached out for her device and opened up the item selection screen. Listed were five items. Underneath them, the numbers.

"My life..."

Her heart pounded heavily, and her breathing roughened. She exhaled, then inhaled. The sounds of her ragged breaths echoed in the empty alley. The ground shook—or was that just her imagination? Snow White couldn't tell. If she took an item, she'd lose part of her life. At the least, that would be three years; at the most, twenty-five. What would La Pucelle do? Her fingers shaking, she clicked PURCHASE. The invisibility cloak that took twenty-five years off her life—with that, she could escape any attacker…possibly.

SOLD OUT!

Sold out?

The words on the screen indicated the item was out of stock. No matter which one she clicked, the same message appeared.

"Aw, I told you, pon. The early bird gets the worm, so you should have bought it fast."

She dropped the magical phone. It bounced and rolled into the steel trash cans behind a restaurant with a clank.

"It's always first come, first served…"

Whatever Fav was saying, Snow White couldn't hear it. She just stared dumbly at her empty right hand.

Weapon, invisibility cloak, energy pills.

Together, Swim Swim, Tama, and the Peaky Angels had three items. They'd tried to buy them all, but the rabbit's foot and four-dimensional bag were already gone.

"We should have looked earlier." "Don't say that, sis."

After hearing from the Peaky Angels about the download items being up for sale, the four had gathered at Ouketsuji. They got Fav to explain the prices of the items, and Swim Swim instantly decided they should purchase them. She instructed Tama to take the weapon and the Peaky Angels to get the energy pills. When the Peaky Angels complained that part of their life span was too expensive, she purchased the invisibility cloak herself.

When a leader takes the initiative and gives up twenty-five years of their life, who would make a fuss about shortening their own life by a few years? Through her actions, Swim Swim demonstrated how necessary this was and moved the other three to action. Yunael ended up paying for the medicine after losing a game of rock-paper-scissors.

They hadn't quite believed Fav's explanation that they'd lose years off their life, but as soon as they bought the items they knew it was true. The moment they clicked the PURCHASE button, a shuddering sensation ran up their spines, as if something had been taken from deep inside. In its place, only a chill remained.

"Swim Swim, aren't you scared of dying twenty-five years earlier?" Tama asked.

"Yes."

"Really? Then why?"

"I'm the leader. It was important."

Swim Swim looked the same as always. No burdens, fear, or hesitation. She was so unperturbed, you'd never guess she'd just lost twenty-five years of her life. It was appalling.

How would Ruler have responded? What would Ruler have done? Ruler had dominated Tama's thoughts recently.

Their old leader had been full of confidence. She'd been smart. Strong. Confidence, brains, strength—Tama possessed none of these, but Ruler had.

She was also the one who'd taught Tama how to be a magical girl. Most who tried to teach her ended up throwing her out halfway through. Kindergarten, elementary school, middle school—the story was always the same. Her teachers either wrote her off as a lost cause, or she graduated before fully grasping the content.

But Ruler hadn't abandoned her. She'd called her an idiot, hit her, and abused her, but still she'd allowed her to stay. Tama's attempts to nuzzle her leg were met with kicks, but she hadn't minded if it meant she wasn't abandoned. The day she'd received her collar, she'd been so happy she ran around the temple grounds and got a scolding for being obnoxious.

She'd assumed Swim Swim thought the same of Ruler—until she suggested a betrayal.

At first, she'd thought it was a joke or something. Or maybe there was some deeper meaning she didn't understand. She remained confused throughout the whole process, until eventually the coup d'état succeeded and Swim Swim became the new leader after Ruler's death. Despite knowing the plan, she hadn't understood it, so the news was a huge surprise to Tama. However, she was in no position to object, and unable to do anything, here she was at Ouketsuji.

"Ohhh, amazing!" "So magi-cool!" "It seems really sharp." "I wouldn't want to be on the wrong end of that."

Swim Swim's weapon resembled a *naginata* pole arm but lacked the distinctive curved blade. Instead, the steel resembled a giant knife. The handle was about a yard long, the blade maybe a foot. It certainly wasn't worth all the praise the angels lavished upon it, and it looked unrefined and awkward. Were they just trying to suck up?

"Whatcha gonna name it?" "The instructions said to give it a cool name, right?"

Swim Swim bowed her head and thought for a while.

"Ruler," she muttered. Unable to discern why she gave it the exact same name as their former leader, the Peaky Angels and Tama all stared at the weapon. It shone in the light of the angels' halos.

Swim Swim had proposed they share the items among themselves. Ultimately, Tama ended up with the invisibility cloak, Swim Swim with the weapon, and the Peaky Angels with the energy pills. The reason Swim Swim wound up with the cheapest item despite paying the most was because she herself requested it. No one dissented.

"Don't you want to use the best item?" Tama asked Swim Swim.

"This weapon goes with my magic. That cloak goes with yours," she said. Then she added, "The Peaky Angels are holding the pills for safekeeping."

Tama wondered what she meant by the cloak "going with" her magic, but couldn't think of a reason. She sort of understood why a weapon suited Swim Swim—she looked best when wielding it, after all. Swim Swim reached out and patted her on the head, as if she thought Tama was troubled instead of attempting to think. Ruler most likely would have yelled at her and called her an idiot. She wasn't sure which she preferred. Maybe one day she would be.

Everyone had to know—even Tama knew, and she was as slow as they come. La Pucelle's accidental death that week meant no one was cut. Then the items had been added. Most of them seemed more appropriate for purposes other than helping people. Swim Swim and the Peaky Angels were raring to go. When she considered what for, Tama shivered.

High-quality furnishings decorated an elegant room: a shag carpet with a complex design, a small ebony desk, a black leather sofa, a gorgeous chandelier, simple watercolor paintings in lavish frames, a three-pronged coat rack, honey-colored candles in a dull-silver candelabra. There was even a pillar and solid wood flooring. *This must be the club's VIP room*, she thought as she surveyed the place.

Calamity Mary inspired as many bad rumors as there were stars in the sky, one of which was that she had ties to a criminal gang. She'd entered the building via the back door and passed smoothly through to this room, ignoring the other guests and getting past the black suits without hassle. Given this, it was hard to deny the stories.

Magicaloid 44 was a robot magical girl. She wore backpack-shaped booster rockets on her back, a weapon rack around her waist, an antireflective hood over her main camera, and various smaller thrusters all over her body for minor adjustments during flight, and her body was made of magicalium alloy that felt like human skin but was harder than steel. If the other magical girls were humans in cosplay, then Magicaloid 44 was a robot made to look human. She was certainly different, that was for sure. Yet none of the staff shrieked in shock or pointed at her. Their expressions hardened, but that was all.

"Your teachings are sinking in, it seems."

"Kissing my ass will get you nowhere."

Calamity Mary chugged the amber liquid filling her Baccarat crystal glass. With her legs spread and her hips sunk into the sofa, she formed the very picture of a gunslinger out of a spaghetti Western.

Magicaloid 44 remembered the post that had made the rounds on the Internet at the beginning of the month about Calamity Mary's assault on the apartment of a Triad gangster. Some reports said she'd acted alone, but the stories that called it a paid hit were more accurate. The compensation would be, say, permission to drink all the expensive alcohol in a high-class club and free rein to use it for her own personal reasons while the staff pretended not to notice anyone she brought with her.

Knowing her, it was quite possible. Their relationship was merely that of veteran and newbie, but even so, she understood that any comments about Calamity Mary's behavior would cost you.

"The items are on sale now," said Magicaloid 44.

"What did you buy?"

"Nothing. I value my life," she answered honestly. No one lied to Calamity Mary.

"So boring. I bought the bag. It seems useful."

"I envy you."

How many times that day had Calamity Mary knocked back a glass of that amber liquid? While Magicaloid 44 remained expressionless on the outside, on the inside she sighed. Magical girls were immune to poison—their physical strength nullified its effects. So obviously they couldn't get drunk off alcohol, yet still Calamity Mary continued to drink. Was it one of her human habits, or just a part of her magical-girl character?

"So, did you give any thought to my proposal?"

"What was it…? You wanted to team up with me?"

"Yes. That is what I said over the magical phone."

La Pucelle's death had meant no one was cut for one week. In other words, if anyone died, she would be the one cut, regardless of candy count. Some most likely considered this method quicker than simply earning candy. It was better to act than wait to be killed.

So far, there was Swim Swim's band of four, Top Speed with Ripple, and Sister Nana with Winterprison. Magical girls were starting to team up more and more, and it was becoming far too dangerous to act alone. The ones still without a group were Snow White; the Magician of the Forest, Cranberry; Calamity Mary; and the new girl. Of those, Magicaloid 44 only had a connection to Calamity Mary, albeit a tenuous one. Mary was also the most reliable in combat.

"I do not mind if you think of me as an errand girl. The only way I survive is if I depend on your power."

"I see."

Calamity Mary stopped drinking and stared into Magicaloid 44's eyes. She seemed to be appraising her, or searching for a hint of a lie. Or maybe she was just staring blankly with no thoughts behind her eyes at all. The room was soundproofed from the outside world, and without even a single ticking clock, it was truly silent. The ice in her glass cracked.

"Y'know, the good thing about you is you always seem ready to stab me in the back."

"Betraying you is an unwinnable game."

"I like how you keep me on my toes. If it's not today, it'll be tomorrow. Or the day after that."

"Please."

Magicaloid 44 laughed, trying to dodge her suspicion, but there was no telling if she actually had. In her head, she marveled.

Calamity Mary was absolutely correct.

Magicaloid's magic changed daily. Each day, she could remove at random from her weapon rack one of 444,444,444 "useful futuristic gadgets" that became usable for that day only. If she could consistently obtain powerful gadgets, she'd never need to team up with anyone. She'd simply destroy all her enemies with ease. But some days she'd end up with items she could not for the life of her understand how to use, like the Fat Removal Manipulator or the Insect Breeding Appraiser. Those were hardly useful. For all her good days, she had equally bad ones, and that was no good.

Calamity Mary was a brutish, violent, irrational, and vulgar woman, but that was most likely the type of magical girl the management was looking for. Under the current rules, those were the

only ones who could survive after the addition of the items. Thus, Magicaloid 44 had to follow suit.

"I'd rather die than partner with a fathead like Ruler or an idiot like Sister Nana. Winterprison and Cranberry I'd rather fight than serve. Snow White should just shut up and die."

Calamity Mary's appraisal of the other girls seemed convincing, at least to Magicaloid 44. The gunslinger was hardly the intelligent or logical type, but she did have experience.

"Then what about me? Magicaloid 44?"

"I guess you could be a good underling. A good servant to your master. You get a passing grade."

"So you will team up with me?"

"If you pass my test, I don't mind letting you watch my back."

"Test?"

"Go kill someone." Joy spread across her face as she imagined something. "Don't worry. If you die instead I'll be sure to avenge you. I'll host the grandest, most extravagant, most breathtakingly bloody massacre in your honor."

Support pole, sign, concrete base—she tore them apart with the ease of a knife through butter. Ripple shredded the steel signs, then chucked the pieces into a basket, one after another. No matter how she threw the steel, it would morph unnaturally and land in the basket, as if it had been sucked in. Her magic, the accuracy of her shuriken, seemed to affect anything she threw with her hands. The rules were surprisingly lax in that regard.

Kitayado locals had been complaining for over a month that the three foreign road signs—complete with concrete around the base, as if they'd been ripped straight out of the ground—had been abandoned in an emergency fire lane. Apparently, there was some confusion about which department was in charge of such matters. Until they were disposed of, they'd just sit there wasting people's time, fanning the flames of their anger, so that night the two magical girls worked to dispose of them.

All that was left to do was leave the pieces marked as unburnable trash at the dump, and their mission would be complete. Once morning came, someone would see it and take care of it. This would most likely net them each one hundred pieces of candy, a large amount in line with the effort required.

"Okay, all ready. Hop on."

"The weight..."

"Hmm?"

"The weight... Will it be okay...?"

"Oh, is that what you're worried about? Naw, no problem!"

The cargo hung from Top Speed's broomstick, Rapid Swallow. Thanks to the additional concrete, the signs might have weighed about the same as a person, though it was difficult to tell. Ripple worried whether the broomstick would still float, but Top Speed easily took flight with Ripple and the remains of the signs in tow.

"I can't go as fast, though. Not because of the weight, but because of the air resistance and stuff. I don't really understand it."

Ripple clicked her tongue.

The broomstick was certainly slower than normal. But that wasn't what irritated her. It was because she was so used to sitting in the back seat that she instantly recognized the slower speed.

They had utterly and unequivocally become a pair. Even the Internet was calling them the witch and ninja duo. Ripple tsked and tightened her grip around Top Speed's waist.

"Don't get so mad."

"I'm not mad..."

"Sure, it sucks we couldn't snag an item. But how many things are really worth paying for with your life span?"

By the time Ripple had learned the items were on sale, they were all sold out. Apparently, the same went for Top Speed. She'd called right away.

"The game's hook was that it was free to play, anyway. This is nothing."

If they were partners, fine. Ripple just wished she could trust her partner more. Top Speed simply wasn't reliable. She kowtowed to Calamity Mary, even groveled, and she couldn't even obtain a single item. Ripple found herself constantly wondering if a mere chauffeur was worth calling a partner.

"We could be killed without one..."

"By who?"

"Another magical girl..."

"Ha-ha! No way. We can always run away if it looks like we're about to die. Who's gonna catch me if I snatch you up and zoom off into the sky?"

"Some of them can fly... Like the angels in the video..."

"Sure, the Peaky Angels and Magicaloid 44 can fly. But there's a huge difference between flying and flying faster than anyone, Ripple. No magical girl can catch me!"

Top Speed grabbed the brim of her hat and pulled it lower. It was impossible to tell her expression from behind, but her tone was terribly light.

"I'm not bluffing or blowing hot air, either. I'm doing this magical-girl thing because I can run away whenever I like. I can't die for at least six more months."

She was constantly going on about those six months, so Ripple constantly asked her what would happen. But she never got a satisfying answer. Maybe she'd find out in six months.

Underneath the moonlight, the broomstick carried its two passengers across the sky.

Snow White spun to look behind her in the empty alley. Fear coursed through her veins, and her ears strained to hear even the tiniest noise. She could have sworn she heard something drop on the asphalt. Maybe it was just her imagination. Practically every day since La Pucelle's death, she'd felt someone nearby and called out, but received no response. Sometimes, she sensed something approaching and lay in wait, but no one ever showed.

Whenever she turned around, no one was there. She knew her nerves were running high, but she couldn't relax. She was too afraid.

Snow White ran.

She darted from alley to alley in the long shadows created by the moonlight. She tried her best to keep out of the light, but after three turns, she heard a noise behind her. Something was rhythmically tapping on concrete. When Snow White stopped, the noise stopped.

Footsteps?

Goose bumps ran up her skin. She turned around to find a pair of eyes staring right back at her. A magical girl she'd never seen before was hiding behind a wall. She had on an apron dress with puffy sleeves, socks, shoes, drawers, and a ribboned headband. She was the spitting image of Alice from *Alice in Wonderland*, but all her clothes were black. The only white thing on her was the creepy plush rabbit under her arm. Her hunched posture reminded Snow White of a predator about to pounce on its prey.

"Finally… I've found you."

Joy shone from within her dull, iris-less eyes, and the corners of her lips twisted upward.

Snow White couldn't move a muscle. One step, two steps, three—the girl slowly drew closer. On the fourth, she was about fifteen feet away. Snow White tried desperately to keep her knees from shaking. After that, the girl stopped.

The black Alice cocked her head. Slowly, ever so slowly, it continued to tilt until, with a pop, it fell off. Where her head had been, Snow White could clearly see her windpipe, her veins, and even her spine. The next second, a geyser of blood showered the small street.

The decapitated body sank to its knees and collapsed on top of its head. Snow White struggled to understand what had just happened. Covered in the black Alice's blood, she stared wide-eyed and unblinking at the convulsing corpse.

"Well, it appears I ended up saving you."

A robot appeared from behind the black Alice's body and stepped over it, seemingly not worried if the blood stained her shoes. She splashed toward Snow White through the pool forming from the headless corpse.

"We have met in chat many times, have we not? I am Magicaloid 44."

She looked exactly like a robot. Her skin was plasticky, her eyes red. Distinctive designs added a magical-girl touch to the mechanical bits on her back, legs, hips, and other places on her body. On her back, she wore a red backpack much like an elementary schooler's.

"Hmm. You know, I imagined I might experience sickness, or uncontrollable shaking, or even ecstasy. Some kind of emotional response. But I only feel disgust, like I did when I was a child and we watched pigs being butchered on that school trip. An instinctual disgust, perhaps."

Her face held no expression, but her tone suggested she was trying to joke.

"This is my first time killing a person...a magical girl, but it is not very interesting. I guess I will never understand why Calamity Mary loves killing so much."

Magicaloid 44 extended her right hand, and Snow White recoiled.

"Can you see it? There are fine threads attached to my fingers. I guess you cannot. Boy, I am glad today's mystery gadget turned out to be useful."

Something glittered in the moonlight, but it was impossible to tell exactly what. Magicaloid 44 swiped her right hand to the side, and without a sound five cuts appeared in the concrete wall next to her. Snow White gasped.

"My plan was to just kill you."

She kicked the head at her feet, sending it rolling over to the other girl. Snow White barely managed to remain standing—if it had landed face up, she surely would have sunk to the pavement. But the face was toward the ground.

"I was not planning to kill someone else. Though this is good-bye for you as well. There is no reason to keep you alive. Maybe Calamity Mary will be more pleased with two bodies instead of one. If murder repulsed me, I would be more careful. But it is no big deal. Well, good-bye."

Magicaloid 44 raised her right hand, and a loud screech erupted, like metal being pierced. Her arm still in the air, the robot looked down to her chest. Something was protruding from it. Someone had impaled her through the chest with an arm. Unable to believe what she was seeing, Magicaloid 44 stared at the arm as it lifted her up and slammed her into the crimson puddle. Blood drenched Snow White and dyed her white clothes almost entirely red.

She'd held it in for a long time, but that was too much. A scream escaped from deep within her throat. Magicaloid 44's impaler was none other than the decapitated black Alice, whose head still lay at Snow White's feet.

Her own scream woke her up. She jumped out of bed, sweating profusely. Her pajamas were soaked and sticky and gross—and not just her pajamas, but her sheets, blanket, and pillow covers, too.

"Koyuki? What's the matter?"

From downstairs, her mother called with worry.

"Nothing!" she answered.

A dream?

She hoped it was only a dream. But it had been too real. Though something like that could never happen in reality, it had. Koyuki glanced down at her right hand. In it she clutched a fluffy white rabbit's foot.

CHAT #4

Fav: So…
Fav: Has everyone mastered their items, pon?
Fav: What? Enough with the formalities, pon? Oh, fine
Fav: This week Magicaloid 44 was cut
Fav: Well, see you next week
Fav: Oh, Cranberry. Thank you for the music, pon

CHAPTER 5
FAREWELL TO THE HINDRANCE

Swim Swim's magical phone rang. Tama fell silent, and even Yunael and Minael stopped chatting to listen to her conversation with Fav. After exchanging a few words, she slipped the phone between her breasts.

"What's the matter? Did something happen?"

"Sister Nana sent a message. She wants to meet."

"Seriously?" "Winterprison is scary." "What do we do?" "What?"

"Above all, deal with strong enemies swiftly."

If they couldn't win in a fair fight, then they would just have to fight dirty. Swim Swim gave the angels her instructions.

Atop the desk sat a lone ball of fluffy white fur. The plethora of plush animals in the room wasn't unusual for a girl to have, but this item was not like the others.

"What is this?"

"The rabbit's foot listed in the game, pon. Something lucky will happen when you're in trouble, pon."

"Why do I have it?"

"Maybe you picked it up after someone dropped it?"

"Who is 'someone'?"

"Logically speaking, probably Hardgore Alice, pon."

"Hardgore Alice?"

"The girl who looks like an all-black version of Alice from *Alice in Wonderland.*"

So it really had happened. Visions of the shambling headless corpse resurfaced. Bile rose in her throat, but she suppressed it. Her heart had never been at peace since La Pucelle died. Every time she remembered her death, the urge to throw up and cry overtook her.

"You won't lose your sanity at least, so don't worry, pon. Business depends on our magical girls remaining healthy in body and mind, pon."

As if he had read her mind, Fav cut off all escape. Anger bloomed in her. She wanted to scream, smash the magical phone, and stamp on the pieces. But she wasn't brave enough to hang up on the only one she could still converse with.

Hardgore Alice had been decapitated and walked away. Such a scene you'd only see in nightmares—yet it had all been real. Her death hadn't been reported in chat, so she was still alive. If the rabbit's foot belonged to her, then what did she think now that Snow White had it? She doubted she would get away with a friendly explanation that she'd picked it up by accident.

"Can't you give this back to her for me?"

"You'd have to do that in person, pon. Fav can contact her for you though, pon."

She'd asked precisely because she didn't want to meet in person, but he didn't seem to understand. Or maybe he did, and he was saying this on purpose. Was it malice she sensed from the black-and-white sphere floating daintily in the air? Or was it indifference?

Snow White collapsed on the desk and cried. Five minutes of sobbing later, she raised her head, a little recovered. She thought about how much easier it would be to just let her mind go.

From the floor below, her mother called, "Koyuki! Dinnertime!"

"Coming!" She stood from her chair. She reached out to turn off the magical phone, but just before she could, Fav piped up, half an octave higher than normal.

"Oh, I have a message, pon."

"Message?"

"Sister Nana wishes to meet you, pon. What do you say, pon?"

Magical girls didn't get many opportunities to meet others like them in person. Of course, if two girls paired up, like Snow White and La Pucelle, Sister Nana and Winterprison, or Top Speed and Ripple, they would naturally see each other. But outside of the mentor system, there weren't any reasons to meet. No major accidents or events that required them to join forces had occurred since they became active in N City. Plus, some girls were more territorial than others, and they were strong enough to maintain their own areas, so there was no real reason for anyone to set foot in another's neighborhood.

Sister Nana had visited other territories—except the late Ruler's—with friendly intentions before, but after Calamity Mary nearly killed her, she had adopted a firm policy of noninvolvement and nonintervention. That is, until this game to reduce the number of magical girls to eight.

Personally, Snow White had only ever met Sister Nana and Winterprison in real life once, before Sister Nana stopped leaving her house.

Snow White arrived early, but Sister Nana and Winterprison were already there. Every time she saw Winterprison, she marveled at how cool she looked. She was more like a prince than a magical girl. As for Sister Nana, she exuded kindness. The solemn abandoned supermarket serving as their meeting place reminded her of a run-down chapel.

"It is good to see you again, Snow White."

"Hey."

"Hello, Sister Nana! Hello, Winterprison!"

"I heard about La Pucelle. It is...truly regrettable..." She clasped Show White's hands and dropped her head.

Tears stung Snow White's eyes. Was she happy that others missed La Pucelle, too, or did remembering La Pucelle's death make her sad? She couldn't rightly say.

Sister Nana raised her head.

"We cannot allow such tragedy to continue. This is the time for us to band together! We can pool our knowledge and find a solution!"

The tears welling in her eyes spilled over. Sister Nana's hands were warm and secure around hers. Everyone she'd met since the start of the game had been hostile, save for La Pucelle. None of them had spared a kind word or needed her. To them, she was no more than prey.

Snow White nodded.

"I want to help... Please, let me help!"

"Oh, thank you, Snow White! Let us work hard together."

Great tears continued pouring from Snow White's eyes, and through her blurred vision she could see Sister Nana smiling. Maybe it was the tears, but her smile looked crooked somehow. Still, it was reassuring. Sister Nana looked away and spoke to some-one behind Snow White.

"What do you say? You left before we could hear your answer the other day."

Had she invited another magical girl? Snow White turned around toward whoever Sister Nana was talking to—and there was Hardgore Alice, a dark parody of her namesake, peeking out from the entrance to the supermarket. Snow White bit back a scream and jumped to hide behind Winterprison. Her hands were still firmly held by Sister Nana's, so she nearly fell over trying to change places with the nun, but nonetheless she moved extraordinarily fast.

"Um... Do you two know each other?"

"Yes, we do."

Hardgore Alice answered before Snow White could tell her about the attack. All the girl in white could do was quiver in fear behind Winterprison. Suspicion darkened the prince-like girl's expression, but Sister Nana continued without concern for Snow White's reaction.

"Um, well then… Will you help us, Hardgore Alice?"

"Yes. I understand. I will help."

Hardgore Alice spoke blankly, like she was reading off a script. Her inelegant speech sounded like a translation of her response from a foreign language.

"Oh, today is such a wonderful day! Thank you so much!"

Apparently Sister Nana didn't doubt her sincerity. She ran over to Hardgore Alice, clasped her hands, and shook them vigorously, just like she had with Snow White.

The last thing Snow White wanted was to end up alone with Hardgore Alice by accident. But Sister Nana's constant delighted exclamations ("We four are united in purpose!") left her no opportunity to tell them the truth.

"I have other meetings with magical girls planned for today. Perhaps our ranks will yet increase," Sister Nana mused happily.

Unable to think of a reason to stop her, Snow White ended up in the one situation she wanted to avoid—alone with Hardgore Alice. She tried to mutter a good-bye and extricate herself, but when she turned she discovered Hardgore Alice following her. Awkwardly, she smiled and bowed, then set off quickly, rounded a corner, and looked back. She was still there. A shiver went up her spine.

Maybe she'd only been playing nice earlier because Sister Nana and Winterprison were there. But with them gone, she probably felt free to attack. Snow White put up her guard, but Hardgore Alice just stared, unmoving, as if her eyes had been glued there.

Oh, right.

Remembering, Snow White reached into her pocket. Her fingers touched soft fur, and she pulled out the rabbit's foot. She held it out to Hardgore Alice.

"Is this yours? Um, I didn't steal it. It was just there when I woke up, honest."

That was the truth, but it seemed like a flimsy excuse. Snow White backed up, still holding out the rabbit's foot.

"No."

"Huh? Am I wrong?"

"That belongs to you."

"N-no, I've never owned something like this."

"I gave it to you. To Snow White. So it's yours."

"Huh? Why? Why would you give it to me?"

Hardgore Alice suddenly cocked her head, startling Snow White. She almost expected her head to fall off again. What exactly had happened the night Magicaloid 44 beheaded her? On closer inspection, there were no scars or bandages on her neck. A natural assumption would be that her magic was responsible, but the power to survive decapitation was too much to believe.

"Because I felt like it."

"Huh?"

"I felt like it, so I gave it to you."

"But why—?"

Hardgore Alice cocked her head again and stared.

"Because I felt like it."

Yesterday, Hardgore Alice had been a blood-covered monster that could move even after death, inspiring a self-explanatory fear. But this Hardgore Alice...this magical girl cocking her head at Snow White...blocked the way as an unfathomable object of terror.

Water gushed from the fountain in the center of the town square in a simple rhythm. The show of flashing lights and changing spray arcs was over. The fountain simply continued its work in a robotic manner—though it was in fact a machine—as if the lively waterworks of only a few minutes ago had never even taken place. The spectators drifted away one by one, abandoning the benches around the fountain, signaling the end of the light show.

Ripple tsked.

Every month on the fifteenth at ten PM, the fountain in N City's central park square hosted a light show. The infrequency of the lovely display made it particularly special—the lights even changed depending on the season, flaring bright pink in April when the cherry blossoms were in bloom and replicating exploding fireworks in August—and ensured more people came to watch.

A bigger audience meant more problems, and more work for a magical girl. All the potential witnesses also lowered the risk of an attack.

Top Speed's plan had seemed sound, so Ripple had agreed. They watched the entire affair from the roof of the park's multipurpose auditorium, completed the previous summer, but not a single problem had cropped up. After enjoying the colorful display, the people quietly left. The only thing the girls had done was dispose of cans, empty convenience store food containers, and broken glass before people showed up.

Had this been Jounan, would there have been more of a disturbance? A fight or two might have broken out in Kubegahama and Kobiki, where fishermen and tradesmen still resided. But nothing of the sort happened in Nakayado. That was what made it Nakayado, after all, and while Ripple liked that aspect, right now what she wanted more than anything was a problem.

The ninja tsked again. Perhaps she should be happy about the peace, but there was no way for her to earn candy.

"Man, good thing nothing happened."

"It's not a good thing..."

"Hmm? Ya say something?"

"No..."

"Wasn't that a pretty sight? The moon was out and everything, so we could see the lights all the way from over here. We shoulda brought some booze to watch it with."

Ripple reached into a Tupperware container, picked out a mushroom with her fingers, and popped it into her mouth. Top Speed could be annoying, but her cooking was always good. The stewed vegetables were juicy with soup stock.

"I can't drink alcohol…"

"Why not?"

"I'm underage…"

"Huh? You mean not just as a magical girl, but for real? In real life? Wow, I just can't see it. Ripple, how old are you actually?"

"Seventeen…"

"Seriously? I'm nineteen."

If Ripple wasn't wrong, a nineteen-year-old was still a minor in their country. Naturally, that meant she shouldn't be drinking. Ripple clicked her tongue.

"So, you're younger than me, huh? I thought you were my age. Maybe older."

She had thought she was older and still used that tone with her? Ripple made her signature sound of irritation and reached out for another stewed veggie. Potato this time. It was good.

"Is school fun?"

"It's whatever…"

"You have friends?"

"No…"

"What about family?"

"No…"

"Man, you seem just like me when I was seventeen. I'm getting déjà vu here. Creepy."

Not many could resist pointlessly acting older once they learned they were talking to someone younger—Ripple thought it was inane, but she didn't tell Top Speed that.

"You're super-honest, though. You answer any question I ask. When I was seventeen, I was more like a knife. Like, anyone who tried to get close got cut. I'm all dull now, though."

Ripple clicked her tongue.

"Ripple, Ripple."

A high-pitched synthetic voice came from her magical phone. Fav turned it on remotely and projected a hologram.

"Fav has a message for you, pon. Calamity Mary wants to meet. She'll be waiting at the Hotel Priestess in Nakayado at eleven PM two days from now, pon."

Ripple looked at Top Speed, and Top Speed looked at Ripple.

"C'mon, Ripple. No need to look so grumpy."

Apparently her distaste showed in her expression. Well, she hated the idea. Hated it a lot. The fear of staring down a gun still hadn't faded, even months later. Sometimes she had nightmares of her death at Calamity Mary's hands.

"I'll pass..."

"Whoa, you'll pass? I know how you feel, but don'cha think something really bad could happen if ya don't go? I'm getting serious bad vibes—my one tiny wish to live another six months might not come true because of this."

"Would you stop that...?"

"Hmm?"

"Tell me why you keep saying six months already..."

"Oh..."

"Hey, Ripple! Ripple!"

From within the projected image, Fav flapped his wing vigorously. So many scales flew off that a yellow cloud seemed to cover the image, nearly blocking him out.

"Calamity Mary says it's important."

Ripple looked at Top Speed, and Top Speed looked at Ripple.

"Seriously, no need to look so grumpy."

Ripple clicked her tongue.

Swim Swim wasn't the only one who knew Ruler had been cautious of Calamity Mary—Tama and the Peaky Angels did, too. "Cautious" was a weak word to describe her attitude, though; perhaps "hated" was more fitting. She'd seen Calamity Mary as an enemy and something in her way.

But despite all this, she had never tried to start a fight with her. The first target she'd chosen to steal candy from was Snow White, not Calamity Mary. Ruler had hated and feared the gunslinger at the same time. Why this was, Swim Swim did not know. The two had become magical girls long before Swim Swim had, so while she could guess what might have happened, she doubted she'd ever truly know. For now, all she knew was that Calamity Mary was scary and nearly untouchable and that Winterprison, who'd gone toe-to-toe with her, was on the same level.

Every magical girl in the city knew how Winterprison had fought Calamity Mary to save Sister Nana. The nun had made sure to brag about Winterprison's strength in chat after.

Ruler was Swim Swim's idol, but also someone to surpass.

And Ruler had feared Calamity Mary above all.

The only one to fight on even terms with Calamity Mary was Winterprison—who would be arriving soon.

If she could beat Winterprison, could she beat Calamity Mary? Surely it wasn't that simple. But possible victory was infinitely better than defeat. Ruler would have thought the same.

Both parties agreed to meet at Ouketsuji. If they didn't manage to win on their home turf, they'd definitely lose their base. But regardless of the risks, she was set on Ouketsuji. It was easier to set up traps in a familiar place, and they had the land advantage if a battle broke out.

That didn't mean they needed to do anything fancy, though. Ruler had never been a fan of complicated things and always insisted that plans be as simple as possible.

Swim Swim peered outside through the skylight. Filtered by the glass, the courtyard appeared faded. Something was moving—a bug? An endlessly chirping autumn insect, or a predatory insect eyeing it for a meal? Between Winterprison's group and hers, which was the predator and which was the prey?

Suddenly the chirping stopped, signaling the arrival of Sister Nana and her companion. Two sets of footsteps creaked across the floorboards in the silent temple. The sound of a door opening followed the creaking, and the two faces appeared in the entrance. Swim Swim's eyebrow rose slightly. Sister Nana was in front. She wasn't supposed to be there.

"It is good to see you again, Swim Swim. Thank you for your candy donation before."

Silently, Swim Swim stood up. She could sense tension from

behind Sister Nana—or, more accurately, from the person behind her. Sister Nana was smiling pleasantly, not perturbed in the slightest.

"Snow White and Hardgore Alice just recently agreed to join us."

Swim Swim took a step forward. Winterprison stayed still. Another step. And another. Finally, Winterprison moved protectively in front of Sister Nana. *There. Perfect.*

"Go."

As Swim Swim gave the signal, Sister Nana screamed from behind Winterprison. Still wary of Swim Swim, Winterprison turned around, and her face froze in horror. Sister Nana shakily pointed at Sister Nana—there were two of them now. The other nun pushed past the first and clung to Winterprison. Dumbfounded and unable to process what was going on, Winterprison took her in her arms—and received a dagger to the chest.

Even with a dagger embedded in her, Winterprison remained calm.

There were two Sister Nanas. One was screaming, the other grinning; one was crying, the other holding a bloody dagger. The Sister Nana with the weapon kicked Winterprison and backed off. Her body began warping. It bent, twisted, stretched, shrunk, and changed color, and after numerous transformations, the second Sister Nana became two angels. They smiled maliciously, not even trying to hide their excitement. That was when she understood how there had been two Sister Nanas, and how that tiny dagger had pierced her sturdy, muscular body.

Winterprison smiled back. Blood running from her mouth, she smiled. Her enemies were fools. Why had they changed back? If they had stayed as Sister Nana, she never could have attacked, even if she knew it was a fake.

One of them had transformed into the magic dagger that now pierced Winterprison's heart. Blood gushed from her chest. She couldn't breathe. Her consciousness dimmed. But she wouldn't die for a few more seconds. She couldn't die just yet.

"Run!" she shouted at Sister Nana, then activated her magic. Walls of earth shot up, breaking through the floorboards—one, two, three, four, five, six, seven, eight. Stirring up clouds of dirt, the barriers struck the ceiling and trapped the angels. It was a prison.

Winterprison closed the gap in one stride. Balling her left fist hard, she drove her hand into the earthen walls and shattered them, crushing one little angel within.

One angel left: the one who had transformed into the dagger.

Winterprison chopped at her, attempting to rip through her neck with her bare right hand. Unfortunately, the blood spray from her first attack got in her eye, and as the blood loss reached a critical level, she just barely missed the timing. Her target inside the prison ducked, and Winterprison chopped through the upper half of the earthen walls. She tried to attack again, but a hole suddenly opened up beneath her and threw off her balance. Swim Swim attacked, chopping off her right arm.

Winterprison watched her limb arc through the air. She remembered how she'd stroked Sister Nana's hair with that hand, those fingers.

She couldn't sense Sister Nana nearby. Fortunately, she seemed to have escaped. Winterprison relaxed. *Please, please be safe*, she prayed, before dropping to her knees and lowering her head.

After Minael had transformed into a dagger, Yunael had held her and hid under the invisibility cloak. She waited until Sister Nana arrived, then shape-shifted into her. With the real thing right in front of her, her disguise was perfect. Then she'd thrown off the invisibility cloak and shown herself to Winterprison.

The events with Calamity Mary had suggested Winterprison would protect Sister Nana no matter what. But if she suddenly had two people to protect, and one even attacked her, surely Winterprison would be too confused to react.

And up until the stabbing, things had worked out perfectly. But then Yunael lost her life in the counterattack, and Sister Nana ran away so quickly, no one spotted her. It was hardly a success.

Minael wailed and clung to the body of a girl about university age. This was Yunael's real form. Tama sobbed next to her, too.

"Yuna...Yuna saved me in the end, didn't she?"

"Mm-hmm. Yeah."

"Yuna...Yuna..."

"Mm..."

Swim Swim's powerlessness weighed painfully on her shoulders. Ruler would have done better. Swim Swim still couldn't measure up. She had to learn from this mistake for next time.

Alcohol didn't serve as a cure-all for long. For one, it was expensive. Two, there were the hangovers. Three, her husband's complaints. Thanks to that, alcohol never really became that magic medicine.

Eventually, her daughter became an outlet for her frustrations. Under the pretext of "discipline," she kicked her, beat her, burned her with cigarettes, and starved her. When she was drunk, the abuse became a wonderful source of stress relief, until her worthless husband ran away with the victim.

She'd enjoyed bullying her daughter because of her own weakness. The weak could only bully the weaker, after all, and her daughter sufficed for that. But it was a stopgap for what she really wanted. Her true wish was to torment someone stronger. The desperate pleas of a swaggering gangster gratified her in a way her daughter never could have.

The strong, the self-important, the beautiful, the clever, the confident—the expressions of the esteemed when they fell to their knees at unstoppable violence! With pleasure like that, she'd never need to touch alcohol again.

A small compact rested on her ebony desk. The little mirror

reflected a woman in her thirties, nearly forty. She was the definition of a middle-aged woman past her prime. A wide smile spread across her face.

She put her hands to her cheeks and shouted, "Calamity Miracle Kuru Kururin! Transform into the magical gunslinger, Calamity Mary!"

Gone was the tired woman in the mirror. Now she had a holster strapped to her left thigh, a sheriff's badge on her breast, a tiny mole under her left eye, thick blond hair extending down to her hips from underneath her ten-gallon hat, voluptuous breasts barely covered by a bikini-style top, a miniskirt exposing practically everything, soft thighs, long legs, and spurred cowboy boots. Popping her shapely hips to one side, she struck a pose. In the mirror now was a beautiful creature.

There was no need to chant or pose while transforming, but in all the anime Calamity Mary had watched as a child, none of the girls could transform without it. Thus, she should do the same. There was no deeper meaning behind it.

Calamity Mary understood her role. She was happy with it. It meant she could shame magical girls, the strongest and most honorable creatures in existence, and crush them underfoot. To her gun belt she attached the four-dimensional bag, containing all kinds of important tools.

Ten minutes had passed since she left the club. She'd ordered Fav to send for Ripple, then made her way to Ripple's designated neighborhood, Nakayado, to meet her. It was currently 10:45 PM. It was almost time.

Japan National Route X, which the locals called "High Road," passed through Nakayado. Like its nickname indicated, the road stood thirty feet above the ground. Traffic law enforcement here was relatively lenient for a public highway, and this, combined with the sparse traffic outside of the New Year's rush, meant that vehicles often raced by at speeds far above the speed limit.

From her perch atop the tallest hotel in the city, the Hotel

Priestess, Calamity Mary watched the road. The cold wind whipped around her cheeks, threatening to blow away her ten-gallon hat, so she pulled it down tighter. Strong winds made sniping difficult, but with Calamity Mary's magic, a regular weapon became an enchanted weapon. Its power, bullet speed, accuracy, and range were all optimal. No amount of wind would matter. The guns also became easier to handle and maintain. Calamity Mary withdrew one of them from her four-dimensional bag.

It was the Dragunov, a sniper rifle developed by Soviet Russia. While its slim design made it easier to transport, the extra kick made it more difficult to actually use. But none of this mattered to someone with her powers. Calamity Mary held the rifle lazily and squeezed the trigger. With semi-auto mode off, she fired bullet after bullet in rapid succession, but each one found its mark in a car. The Dragunov, designed for urban warfare, was sold for its ability for quick fire.

An explosion, then a fiery plume. One by one, she destroyed the cars on High Road. A flaming tire rolled across the road. When the vehicles erupted into flames, the ones behind them slammed into the blazing wreckage, and so did the ones behind them. The Dragunov picked off the vehicles lucky enough to escape the pileup. The night road was as bright as day.

One man managed to stop his car and jump out in a panic, and she shot him for sport. She thought his guts would explode all over the asphalt, but the truth was far harsher. He didn't just explode—he was erased. Everything above the kneecaps gone without a trace.

A sniper rifle was too powerful as an antipersonnel weapon. It was no fun. Cars were better game than people.

And magical girls were even better.

If she took Ripple on directly, Top Speed would interfere. And if Top Speed fled at full speed, Mary would have no way to catch up. If she wanted to fight Ripple, she had to give her a reason. A noble do-gooder would show up to defeat the evil woman destroying her city and its innocent civilians.

Angering Ripple also made her happy. Two birds, one stone. And after she'd slaughtered Ripple, the town would be crawling with people looking for help—the perfect chance to earn candy. Calamity Mary pulled the trigger until the magazine was empty, destroying everything on the highway.

This was all because of one mistake. If Ripple had just bowed her head the first time they'd met, she would have killed her and that would have been the end of it. But she hadn't, and now Calamity Mary was obsessed. It was all Ripple's fault.

Calamity Mary could not abide those who did not fear her.

CHAPTER 6
MAGICAL CANNON GIRL

A magical phone displayed the flaming highway.

"This is bad… We have to help!"

"I'll follow you, Snow White."

"R-right! Let's go together!"

A magical phone displayed the flaming highway.

"Wh-wh-what do we do? We have to help!"

"Let the other magical girls handle this."

"Huh? But…"

"We'll attack anyone who tries to help. Tama, Minael, hurry and get ready."

"Huh? Huh? Huh?"

A magical phone displayed the flaming highway.

"What's this? Master, you're not going, pon? You should be able to have lots of fun if you do, pon."

"Perhaps."

"You're hard to understand, pon."

"That's enough of that. More importantly, is it true that Winterprison is dead? Who killed her?"

"You should probably consider your future and not some dead rival, pon."

"I just want to know."

The moment she spotted the figure aiming a gun at the highway, her brain exploded with rage. Springing off the broomstick, she dived. Top Speed shouted something, but she couldn't hear it.

"Took you long enough, little girl."

Discarding the rifle, Calamity Mary pulled the pistol from her hip holster and aimed at Ripple as she landed. Silhouetted against the flames of the highway, her eyes were unreadable in the shadows, but her mouth was another story. White teeth flashed in the darkness.

A bullet shot from the pistol. Holding her blade in typical ninja fashion, Ripple deflected it into the sky. Calamity Mary fired again, but she repelled that as well. Boiling rage had completely replaced her fear of the firearm.

Calamity Mary pulled out another pistol with her left hand. With dual weapons, she unleashed a barrage of bullets. They all zipped past Ripple—or maybe it was more accurate to say she dodged them. The slugs were heavy and fast, but she could read their trajectory. And in her hands, a sword was faster.

Tossing away her pistols, Calamity Mary stuck her hand into the bag hanging from her hip. Ripple dashed forward and slashed as she passed, aiming for the carotid artery.

Sparks flew. Her blade screeched against something steel. Ripple turned around and adjusted her stance. Underneath her armpit,

Calamity Mary was holding an automatic rifle about a yard long with a foot-long bayonet.

That was what her blade had struck.

"I guess a Tokarev isn't enough to take out a little girl of your caliber."

Ripple leaped and slashed at her side, but the bayonet rebuffed her blade again. She'd been able to cut through road signs and masses of concrete with no problem, but Calamity Mary's bayonet was a different story. Was she also reinforcing it with magic?

So what if she is?

Tensing her legs, Ripple swung at her torso with all the speed she could muster. Blocked. She shifted her weight and followed up with a stab. Blocked again. Jumping back, she threw three shuriken, but the bayonet denied them all. She feinted to the side and slipped in close to her opponent's breast. The moment she tried to stab between her ribs, she felt intense heat on her face and sailed backward. The butt of the automatic rifle had connected with her face. She rolled to avoid the subsequent fire and, blood streaming from her nose, adjusted her stance again to close the gap quickly.

It was about thirty feet to her target. She traced an arc to the right. One, two, three steps—then a distinctive *click* came from below. Ripple froze. Upon close inspection, the concrete block under her foot was slightly sunken. As she realized exactly what she'd stepped on, a chill ran up her spine.

"Ha-ha-ha… Hya-ha-ha-ha-ha-ha-ha!"

Calamity Mary burst into laughter.

"Go ahead and move your foot, little girl! You'll be in everyone's way if you stand there forever! Die and take the land mine with you!"

The automatic rifle spit a burst of flame. Ripple couldn't lift her right foot or the mine would explode. No normal antipersonnel weapon could hurt a magical girl, but this was a magical trap set by Calamity Mary.

Ripple could no longer move, but bullets rushed at her just the same. She drew the weapon hidden up her sleeve—a ninja blade half the size of her regular one, about the size of a short samurai sword but much better suited to blocking than a full-length blade. Using both swords, she deflected the hail of bullets. Eventually, the automatic rifle ran out of ammo before it could fatally wound her. Calamity Mary pulled the trigger, but only clicks came out.

She chucked the automatic rifle aside.

"Do not go against me."

She shoved her hand into the bag again and pulled out eight items.

"Do not give me trouble."

Attached to each dark green spheroid was a pin. Calamity Mary hooked her finger around it, pulled, and tossed the object at Ripple.

"Do not piss me off."

Calamity Mary flipped over the railing. A fall from the roof of a building was no problem for a magical girl. But for Ripple, there was no escape. If she moved her foot the mine would go off, but if she waited the grenades would explode.

The air boomed.

Something slammed into her, and suddenly she was being pulled through the air. The impact to her side was enough to break her hip, or so it felt. Flames licked at her hair, singeing the ends. Ripple soared through the sky, leaving behind eight grenades and one land mine.

"Enough with the crazy stunts!"

Ripple twisted herself to see the person holding her up, and there was Top Speed, angrier than a hornet's nest.

She'd flown fast as she could, nabbing Ripple from the side just before the grenades exploded. This simultaneously removed Ripple's foot from the mine and set it off, but Rapid Swallow was faster than the explosion. In the end, Ripple had escaped with only a few scorched hairs.

Ripple grabbed Top Speed's shoulder, flipped onto the broomstick, and plopped into the rear seat. That moment, she spotted the brilliant crescent moon in the night sky. Her mind flashed back to

Calamity Mary's smile, glinting white, and she ground her teeth in frustration.

"We have to get rid of her."

"Don't talk like a gangster, yo. We should withdraw."

"Do you know why she was terrorizing the highway? Because she wanted to make me mad. Because she knows I care for this town. She'll continue to hunt here until I die or something stops her. I—"

She took a breath. Why did Ripple want to fight? Because she was angry. Pissed. When Ripple had been Kano Sazanami, most of her motivation had come from anger. Why was she angry now? Was it because of Calamity Mary?

Ripple had always thought the laid-back nature of Nakayado clashed with her own personality. But just thinking about what had happened to her town made her insides boil.

"I don't want to save the world, and I don't even think I can. But...I wouldn't be a magical girl if I turned tail and ran from the people of Nakayado. Even passing strangers."

Ripple squeezed her arm around Top Speed's waist. The heroines she'd idealized long ago surfaced in her mind.

"I am a magical girl."

Top Speed seemed to be at a loss for words. After a while, she let out a breath. This wasn't a sigh or a simple exhalation, though.

"Oh yeah?"

She dipped her chin and pulled down the edge of her triangle hat.

"Well, aren't you proud of yourself."

The broomstick slowed, until finally it stopped.

"I've never seen ya talk so much before," she said, grinning wryly. "But you missed something."

She spun 180 degrees in the air. Ripple held tightly to Top Speed's waist to keep from falling off, but Top Speed didn't sway in the slightest.

"I'm a magical girl, too, ya know."

Boosters extended from either side of the broomstick. Flames ignited within, and they took off like a rocket. The loud flapping of

Top Speed's coat in the wind and their own screeching through the air threatened to destroy Ripple's ears. Not even the sound of the streamlined windshield cutting through the air could catch up. Atop the broom, the girls lay as low as possible to hide behind the barrier.

Thanks to her magically enhanced eyes, Ripple spotted the Hotel Priestess. The roof was gone without a trace, exposing the top floor. Smoke rose from fires here and there. Steel beams jutted out at every angle, and debris covered the floor. She prayed no one had been staying there.

But the sight of her enemy erased all noble prayers from her mind and sent her rage into overdrive. There she stood against one of the ruined hotel walls, watching them. Calamity Mary. Dual-wielding automatic rifles, she opened fire in their direction.

Ripple's magically enhanced eyes could pinpoint each bullet as it traveled through the air, but most of them ended up ricocheting off the windshield. The few that didn't missed by a wide margin and disappeared behind them. Rapid Swallow's windshield possessed formidable strength, able to withstand even supersonic speeds. Calamity Mary seemed to shout something, but the wind carried her voice away, so Ripple had no idea what it was.

The broom made a beeline for Calamity Mary.

It broke through walls and ripped up the floor. The shock wave behind them crossed the entire floor, picking up flames, smoke, carpets, beds, and heavy chunks of rubble in its wake. Six miles away from the hotel, they turned. Then the sound caught up with them, and the mountain of rubble collected by the shock wave dropped out of the sky. A great I-shaped scar was now carved across the entire top floor of the hotel.

Ripple saw everything. Calamity Mary had escaped. She had shot at them until the very last second, but when her bullets couldn't harm Rapid Swallow's armor, she'd turned to the side and dived into the pile of rubble.

Heavy, sticky bloodlust blacker than night coiled around the hotel. It was so thick, they could almost see it. The pile of rubble collapsed, and a silhouette rose from the debris.

"She's alive."

"Looks like…"

"All right, I'm going in for another pass, damn it! Hold on tight!"

Top Speed reignited the boosters, and the armored broomstick rocketed toward Calamity Mary on the hotel. Calamity Mary reached into her bag and pulled out a gun. This was no pistol, nor an automatic rifle—was it a sniper rifle? The barrel was long, about three feet by itself…maybe a little over four feet in total. *She still has more?*

Calamity Mary aimed at them, and her lips twisted. She was smiling. A shiver ran up Ripple's spine, just like when she'd stepped on the land mine.

"Dodge!"

She shouted and lunged forward, grabbing Top Speed's triangle hat and shoving her down with all her might. Rapid Swallow's trajectory jerked to the lower right. The boosters reversed, pumping flame in the opposite direction, but it was too late. They smashed through the hotel wall and floor, and the sudden change in momentum sent them weaving back and forth like a squirming snake until they landed on an office building a few miles away.

The office building was around the same height as Hotel Priestess. And they hadn't so much landed as crashed straight through the roof and destroyed it. Shattered concrete flew everywhere, and clouds of fine glass hung in the air.

"What the hell was that for?"

Top Speed's anger was natural, but Ripple pointed at the top of the windshield.

"Look…"

"Huh?"

The upper section of the windshield was twisted and ripped away. Thousands of bullets and pieces of concrete traveling at supersonic speeds hadn't even scratched it, but now it was beyond repair.

"What happened?"

"That last bullet grazed it…"

Top Speed hadn't seen it because Ripple had shoved her head down. The bullet from Calamity Mary's sniper rifle should have hit the windshield dead-on, but since they had dodged out of the way, it only grazed the top. Yet that was all it took to rip their protection from the broomstick. A direct hit would have ripped through both of the girls.

"How? Her little peashooter wasn't even scratching it earlier!"

"She changed guns…"

That last bullet was clearly faster than the rest. If they hadn't changed direction before she pulled the trigger, they would never have been able to dodge it. It would have scored a bull's-eye, blowing them to smithereens.

Top Speed used Rapid Swallow to stand. Dusting herself off, she placed her triangle hat back on her head and glared angrily toward Hotel Priestess.

"Damn it! Let's go in for another run!"

"If we do the same thing…she'll just shoot us down and kill us."

"So what do we do? I can't do anything except attack head-on!"

"That's all I can do, too…"

"Then what?"

Ripple's direct assault on Calamity Mary had nearly gotten her blown up.

Top Speed's direct assault had nearly gotten them shot out of the sky.

One-on-one, they stood no chance against her. Luck was the only reason they were alive. If they repeated their approach, they'd certainly die this time.

"Next time…"

"Next time?"

"We should take her head-on anyway…"

Calamity Mary's magic was the ability to imbue weapons with power, so she could not create weapons from nothing. She required premade weapons to work her magic. The Dragunov, the Tokarev, the AK, and this KSVK anti-materiel sniper rifle—all of Russian or Soviet Russian make—created an odd contrast with her Wild West gunslinger motif, however.

She would have liked to use only American models, but the South American drug cartels sold mainly black market models. She hadn't exactly been overjoyed when she'd first received them, but now she loved each and every one. Calamity Mary slid her tongue along the muzzle brake. It tasted of iron.

The shot from the KSVK had only grazed the enemy. A narrow miss, but they must have sustained some damage regardless. Even through her rage, she knew her baby's firepower.

Ripple and Top Speed must have learned by now that challenging her head-on without a plan would only lead to their deaths, so what would they do next? People who couldn't win one-on-one usually relied on the advantage of numbers. Most likely, Top Speed would come from the front. But after witnessing the power of the KSVK, she would charge without much speed or power. That would just be the distraction. Ripple would strike from the left, the right, or behind—some angle different from Top Speed's. That would be the real attack. If she could predict that, she could deal with them.

The wide roof was no longer flat. Her battlefield was now covered in rubble. Setting traps was a simple matter. She had had plenty of time earlier, after Top Speed's rescue.

There was no way for Ripple to come straight at Calamity Mary, regardless of the direction she chose. She'd laid down piano wire around the roof and even set up a trap with wire and stun grenades in the room below. If the worst happened and she decided to attack from below, it'd be no problem at all.

Ripple's only opening was from above, but she couldn't fly. Without Top Speed's help it would be impossible, and if Top Speed helped her they couldn't try the pincer attack. She'd easily vaporize them with her KSVK.

Seventy degrees to her right, a window broke in the five-story building—a department store, if memory served—and something large crept out. Calamity Mary had of course noticed, her senses heightened and attention focused, but she was also confused. *Thing* was the only word she could use to describe whatever had climbed out. Seeing it, she couldn't tell what it was. By the time she realized the black, fifteen-square-foot wall was a fire door, she'd pulled the trigger. The fire door blew away, and the flying broomstick lurking behind it zoomed off into the building's shadow.

What was that?

The fire door, most likely from inside the department store, had been mounted on the front of the broomstick. They seemed to be using it as a shield or screen of some kind, but would it do any good? Another fire door popped up in a different window and headed straight for her.

Calamity Mary licked her lips, though they weren't dry. In fact, they glistened with moisture. The moment her tongue poked out of her mouth, saliva dripped from the corner of her lips. She did nothing to stop it.

The fire door was heading straight for her. Last time, she'd been confused and had shot without thinking, but this time was different. She'd fire once she had a clear view of the target.

Come on, little girl.

Come from whatever direction you want.

Then...

Die.

The bullet hit the instant she pulled the trigger. The speed of the bullet far surpassed any magical girl's reflexes. She couldn't have dodged.

The fire door shattered and fell to the ground below. Glee spread across Calamity Mary's face. Then her expression twisted. Not with joy—with bewilderment. The door had exploded, but there was no corpse, not even the remains of the broomstick. There was nothing but the fire door.

The hairs on the back of her neck stood up. She could sense a piercing intent to kill. Tossing aside the KSVK, she pulled the Tokarev from its holster.

She'd already calculated every possible route of attack in case of a diversion—left, right, behind, and below. Even if she was caught unawares, her quick shooting would handle the rest.

She pointed the Tokarev toward the murderous aura she'd sensed—above her. The crescent moon. The starry sky. Wait, were there that many stars before? Not in the middle of town, at least. Flying toward her were thousands of…shuriken? No, too many. The projectiles glittering under the moonlight were not shuriken—but shards of glass. These buildings were full of it.

High above, Top Speed and Ripple gazed down at her from atop the broomstick.

Damn them!

She squeezed three shots off but couldn't manage a fourth. She swiped at the shards with her pistol, and that was it. Glass pierced her shoulder and lower neck, and spinning shuriken ripped through her flesh. A knife sank deep into her forehead and threw her head back, bending her whole body backward.

Don't look down on me! Calamity Mary thought just before she died.

Calamity Mary toppled back, her body riddled with shuriken, knives, and shards of glass. Her ten-gallon hat floated through the air, landing on its owner's breast.

Ripple let out the breath she'd been holding. Pain spread like fire throughout her body. She hadn't had the time to feel it before, but now it hit her full force. She could feel her consciousness fading.

The fire doors had been Ripple's work. By throwing them with her magic, she knew they were sure to fly in a straight line toward Calamity Mary. From the front, the second had looked the same as the first. The point was to make Calamity Mary think Ripple was still using the door as a shield. The moment the violent gunslinger shot at the door, it created an opening for Top Speed and Ripple to attack from Rapid Swallow above.

Once she saw out of the corner of her eye that Calamity Mary had detransformed, Ripple collapsed. It felt like she might stop breathing altogether.

"Nice job, partner."

She raised her head. There was Top Speed, extending her right hand to Ripple as she gasped on the ground. She grabbed it.

"You look like someone used you for target practice. Everything okay?"

"Somehow…"

She pulled the other girl's hand, but for some reason Top Speed collapsed onto her, and Ripple ended up supporting her instead. Before she could ask what was wrong, she noticed the silhouette behind Top Speed.

There stood a girl about high school age, sporting a white school swimsuit and wielding a giant pole arm–hatchet hybrid. The ridiculous outfit and obviously aggressive stance made her intentions clear. Ripple rolled, still holding Top Speed. The massive weapon cut through the floor like a hot knife through butter and scooped up after her. However, Ripple had already sprung into a crouch and whipped out her sword. She parried, and the weapon skipped away to the side. She followed with an immediate slash back at its wielder's left thigh and right wrist.

She should have seriously wounded her, but the girl hardly reacted and continued to swing her weapon as if she didn't notice. Ripple retreated a step. Not a drop of blood appeared where she'd struck.

Magic…?

Dodging a swipe along the ground, Ripple drew her short sword and hurled it. The sword nailed the girl's foot to the hotel floor, but then slipped right out. Still no blood. In fact, she didn't seem to be a wounded at all.

She attacked like a bladed whirlwind, striking with pinpoint accuracy at her enemy's vitals. The girl wasn't even trying to dodge. Direct hits had no impact. Everything felt like whiffs. Her opponent's attacks were heavy and simple. Ripple had no trouble dodging them, but none of her own attacks were finding purchase.

The swimsuit-clad girl retreated, as if realizing they were at a stalemate, and the giant weapon vanished. Then she sank into the hotel floor—first her ankles, then her calves, thighs, and hips, until even her head had vanished.

Ripple clicked her tongue. Her attacks hadn't missed—they'd

passed through her. The girl was definitely using some kind of magic. And as long as she couldn't get around that, Ripple could never win with her abilities.

As the futility of the situation sank in, exhaustion settled heavily on her shoulders. There was nothing to gain from fighting anymore. They'd simply lose. If the girl had retreated, that was fine, but that was an optimistic assumption. It was smarter to assume she was hiding, waiting to strike again, and she had to act accordingly.

Ripple spun around to grab Top Speed and beat a hasty retreat. Suddenly, she stopped.

The one lying facedown on the floor was supposed to be Top Speed. There she was, with her coat declaring "No Gratuitous Opinions" draped across her like a blanket. But the girl wasn't Top Speed. The coat was there, but the triangle hat and witch clothes were gone.

Staggering, Ripple made her way over and kneeled next to the human lying there. She appeared to be in her late teens with braided chestnut hair. A deep wound crossed from her shoulder to her breast, the worst of the bleeding already past. Her eyes were closed, and her expression was so peaceful she might have been sleeping.

Ripple took the girl's hand in her shaking one. It was cold.

The girl was wearing a maternity dress. Her belly was quite large.

Top Speed had always said she needed six more months to live. Ripple bit her lip. Hard. The taste of iron filled her mouth, and blood dripped out, but she didn't release the pressure.

Her words echoed endlessly, deep in Ripple's heart.

Why? Why? Why? Why? Why?

That night, Ripple lost her one and only friend.

The moment the angel descended, Snow White breathed a sigh of relief. Even in these extraordinary circumstances that forced them to fight one another, magical girls rushed to help when disaster struck, regardless of faction. That was how magical girls should be. That was what this was all about.

The Peaky Angels had attacked her and La Pucelle on the steel tower in Kubegahama, and she still remembered them with fear. But if this one wanted to help save lives, then she had to forget the past and assist her. She had to be careful to keep her smile natural, so as not to put her on guard.

As she welcomed the newcomer with the warmest smile she could muster, Hardgore Alice tackled her and sent her rolling across the pavement. Surprised and confused, she stood up and frantically tried to piece together what had happened, only to find Hardgore Alice already in heated battle with the angel.

The angel's expression was not normal. Her lips formed a thin line, her face was pale, her brows were knit, and she was moaning. Hardgore Alice hurled her plush animal onto the road, unceremoniously yanked a traffic sign out of the ground, raised it above her head, and swung. The angel maintained her distance.

What's going on? Snow White wondered. A giant pileup had occurred on the highway, and the casualties were sure to be great. There was so much for the magical girls to do. Yet the angel had attacked her without a thought to the flaming vehicles, the toppled truck, and the countless injured.

Snow White quivered with anger, not fear. She was indignant that this girl could be so selfish and think nothing of others' lives. Her magic let her read the minds of people in trouble to figure out what was wrong, and she could hear countless voices. She knew exactly where each one was, too. It was unbelievable that someone with their powers could just ignore them to fight. Maybe she was the only one who could hear, but it was obvious that people needed help. Could they not see, or did they not care?

The voices in her head were increasing and intensifying. Suddenly, Snow White noticed something. A strange voice was mixed among the cries for help.

Oh no… What do I do?

The source was thirty feet behind her. She looked, but there was no one there.

Swim said to attack them.

But shouldn't I be helping with the accident?

Still, Swim did say...

Maybe I should just take her out, then go help...

"Is someone there?"

Huh? Can she see me? That's not good... How can she see me?

"Are you a magical girl, too?"

The voice stopped.

"Sorry! She found me!"

A dog-eared girl suddenly appeared out of nowhere.

"What are you doing? The plan was for me to act as a distraction while you took her out! You let her find you! Idiot! Stupid dog! Useless!"

The angel lashed out, frantically dodging the road sign.

"If you're not going to use it, then give it to me!" she spat. She spiraled through the air, snatched a transparent cloak from the other girl, tossed it over herself, and disappeared. The dog-eared girl watched her go with tears in her eyes. Snow White and Hardgore Alice, still brandishing the road sign, turned to face her, and she let out a noise that was part shout, part scream, and part cry. She swiped at the ground below her, and a hole a few feet wide opened up below. She dropped into it and disappeared.

Hardgore Alice had served as both her reinforcements and her savior that night. The angel was gone, and the dog-eared girl had turned tail. Snow White limply dropped her raised fist.

"...Let's go help some people, even if it's just us."

"Yes. Understood."

Hardgore Alice set off in search of her rabbit plush, found it in the shadow of some rubble, and picked it up. With her rabbit in her right hand and the street sign slung across her shoulder, she followed after Snow White.

She shut off the TV. The accident on National Route X showed how gruesome things had truly become, but she felt no urge to rush over. If she went, she could do many things to help. But there was nothing she wanted to do.

Sister Nana…Nana Habutae hadn't moved from her bed since she had fled Ouketsuji.

Shizuku Ashu. Weiss Winterprison.

Still on her belly, Nana moved only her face to the side. In front of her was the corkboard displaying the smiling photos of Sister Nana and Winterprison—of Nana Habutae and Shizuku Ashu. Shizuku had always been so kind. Cleaning, laundry, she did it all. She'd helped Nana with a report for university, and even called her cute.

Nana knew her outward appearance was only temporary. People had always called her cute to make fun of her, or to express some sense of superiority, but never had anyone truly meant it. But Winterprison wasn't like them. Whatever it was she'd liked about Nana, her claims that it was "love" didn't seem fake, at least. Maybe she just had bad taste.

Sister Nana had the ability to draw out the power of other magical girls. With her magic, Winterprison became stronger.

She'd cared about Nana quite a bit, but how did Nana feel? No, Nana didn't return the feeling. She loved Winterprison. She'd loved her, but not really cared about her. After all, she'd led her to her death. She was a siren, leading her into danger.

Winterprison…

No matter how many times she thought about it, she arrived at the same conclusion. She was tired of thinking. Had it been hours, or had it been days? Her sense of time was long gone, and she couldn't tell. Nana got up from the bed. Her joints groaned.

Nana was neither kind nor pure. She was conniving when it came to getting what she wanted, and only ever acted with her own best interests in mind. She was neither kind nor pure, but wanted to be seen as such by others. By Winterprison. By her dream prince.

The long scarf hanging from the chair must have been Shizuku's. She doubted it was part of Winterprison's magical-girl outfit. Nana picked up the scarf and chair.

If she'd told Winterprison that she wanted to die as a kind, pure heroine while protecting her prince, what would she have thought? Examining herself now, she could only conclude that was what she had wished for. A sense of loss overtook her sadness.

Placing the chair under the curtain rail, she stood on top of it. She tied the scarf to the rail, then formed a loop.

She had failed to become the heroine who died to save her prince.

She could have become a heroine that avenged her prince. If she'd teamed up with Snow White and Hardgore Alice, she could have magnified their power to assist the suffering people in that giant pileup. But she didn't care.

She slipped the looped scarf around her neck.

She'd failed to save her prince and die, and she didn't want to fight to avenge her prince. The only option left was to follow her prince in death.

Had Winterprison realized Sister Nana's feelings? She'd probably foreseen that Sister Nana would abandon her to escape. Yet still she'd fought and died to protect her.

Sister Nana could never do the same.

And with that impassable rift between them weighing on her mind, Nana kicked the chair out from under her.

CHAT #5

Fav: So, uh, about this week's cuts, pon
Fav: There are a lot more than usual, pon
Fav: Please pay attention so you don't miss any, pon
Fav: Weiss Winterprison
Fav: Calamity Mary
Fav: Sister Nana
Fav: Top Speed
Fav: Yunael
Fav: The above have all been cut, pon
Fav: The remaining magical girls are:
Fav: Swim Swim
Fav: Snow White
Fav: Tama
Fav: Hardgore Alice
Fav: Minael
Fav: Musician of the Forest, Cranberry
Fav: Ripple
Fav: Seven, in total
Fav: Ohhh! We did it! We're finally below the initially proposed eight girls! Wonderful, pon!
Fav: But unfortunately…this isn't the end, pon
Fav: Those items you all received
Fav: have depleted our stores of mana again, pon

Fav: My, what a miscalculation, pon
Fav: So Fav must apologize to all of you
Fav: but the limit of eight is now down to four, pon
Fav: Do your best to earn candy until there are only four left, pon
Fav: Fav knows you all have what it takes to survive, pon
Fav: Well, good-bye~

CHAPTER 7
CRANBERRY'S SECRET

The chaos of Calamity Mary's attack was ultimately explained as an act of terrorism. No groups claimed responsibility for it, but it was the only justification the world might accept.

Snow White and Hardgore Alice worked themselves to the bone helping people, leaving far more than a few witnesses. Additionally, the many weapons Calamity Mary had left behind lent credence to the terrorism story. No one, at least publicly, suspected a magical girl to be the perpetrator, partly because no one could imagine a lovely girl with superpowers as a gun-wielding soldier. Their existence was hardly public knowledge, despite the number of witness reports. Of course, the syndicate that had supported Calamity Mary knew who was behind the attack, but they kept silent. Most likely they didn't spare a thought for what a magical girl was supposed to be. They were just relieved to be free of the nuke waiting to go off.

"My, what an exhausting morning, pon."

The white section of the sphere's body was dull, and the butter-fly wing beat weakly. At least, so it seemed.

"They're calling it a scam, a hoax, fraud, lies, and all sorts of things, pon. Maybe it was too much to hope they'd believe we had to cut down to four just because we added the items, pon."

"If they don't believe you, then so be it."

"Master."

"Yes?"

"You don't think it's okay for Fav to suffer just because it's Fav, do you, pon?"

"It's your job to be hated."

Lying on the bed, Cranberry put a hand to her cheek.

"So please, let them hate you. I have a lot to think about in the meantime."

Several of their number had already died: Nemurin, Ruler, La Pucelle, Magicaloid 44, Weiss Winterprison, Sister Nana, Yunael, Calamity Mary, and Top Speed. It was a shame she wouldn't get a rematch against Winterprison. She'd been so sure Winterprison would be the last one alive.

The game had passed its halfway point, and the most qualified contender, Winterprison, was out. Of those left, maybe Swim Swim or Ripple were most capable. Or perhaps Hardgore Alice. Cranberry preferred interesting opponents.

"Oh, one more thing."

"What is it?"

"Fav was going to make a progress report. Did you have anything specific to add, pon?"

The Magical Kingdom would periodically hold selection tests in order to find new blood. Capable candidates were chosen to compete, and one would be chosen to join their ranks.

As per custom, the selection test curators were called "masters." After the Magical Kingdom dispatched the necessary members, they would adopt the role of adviser and seek out humans from the land the test was being held in, offer words of wisdom, and keep the test proceeding smoothly. Without a master to handle this role, the selection test could not take place.

The special phones provided to masters came preinstalled with

various applications not found on normal magical phones in order to make the test as smooth as possible. Fav, who resided inside this supervisor phone, would obtain whatever items the master required. Fav was also an impish creature, and many of the apps he installed were alarming.

"Fill out the report as you see fit."

"Yes, yes."

Cranberry wondered if Fav would actually do as she said. The idea was to convince the Magical Kingdom that they were carrying out a perfectly normal personnel training session. It had to present their bloodstained death match as a test of peaceful, goody-two-shoes girls.

The Magical Kingdom sought talented individuals, but they would not accept applicant deaths in the name of this pursuit. They claimed it was wrong to disrupt other realms for their own gain.

Of all the idiotic ideas. Cranberry spat.

Reaching out to other realms for talent was a disruption in and of itself. All that crap about making the least possible disturbance was just their hubris talking. If they were going to come in and throw things out of balance anyway, then they might as well use everything at their disposal to achieve their goal. If they wanted talent, then they needed to purge the weak and pick from the strong.

An accident had occurred during the selection test that had made Cranberry a resident of the Magical Kingdom. One of the applicants had attempted to summon a demon in a basement, and it went berserk. By the time she'd subdued the demon, it had killed everyone except Cranberry: her fellow applicants, the supervisor who'd stepped in to help—twelve casualties in total. A great tragedy.

One by one, her classmates had been crushed, melted, mashed, and broken. Cranberry had been nine at the time, so it was a shocking experience for her, but the joy she'd experienced was even greater. Trading blows with violence incarnate, drooling with the elation of slaughter, firing off magic—then, when they were both at wits' end, emerging dominant over her opponent. Truly, that was the definition of a warrior of justice. In defeating powerful enemies, she found catharsis.

The demon purged, she'd stood there intoxicated. Ecstasy coursed through every fiber of her being. She bathed in the joy of overflowing blood until a hologram rose up from the supervisor's phone and asked, "How long are you going to keep standing there, pon?"

The real shock came when she heard it had all been because of an accident. The true selection process seemed so tepid, exasperating, and boring. The failures would laugh with embarrassment, and everyone would celebrate the winner together. But that wasn't how it should be, she thought. It was all wrong. They should be stealing irreplaceable treasures from one another, killing, being killed—and only by surviving to the end did the winner get chosen. That was how things should be.

When she told Fav this, he had answered, "Then you should become a master, pon." Taking his advice, she did just that. Fav admitted he was bored with the current system and eagerly looked forward to a more entertaining selection test under Cranberry's supervision.

She wondered if something inside her had broken during the accident. But it was of no concern to her. As a master, she could conduct the game as she saw fit. As long as the Magical Kingdom never caught wind, she could do as she pleased.

"I just wish I could have enjoyed this as a participant. C'mon, can't I get an invitation?" she muttered to herself.

Swim Swim pondered the situation.

The number of magical girls had been reduced to seven, yet they were given another quota. In order to ensure everyone in her group survived, three other girls would need to drop out of the race. Tama had come scurrying back after her skirmish with Snow White and Hardgore Alice, but Minael was still missing. She didn't seem to be dead, though.

Their ambush had failed because even though Minael had successfully distracted the enemy, Tama had been discovered while wearing the invisibility cloak. It must have been the work of magic.

That magic that let its user find people. That made the invisibility cloak utterly useless. It also meant Tama couldn't hide in a hole for a surprise attack, and if Swim Swim dived beneath the ground, she'd be found anyway. Snow White might even be able to sniff out Minael while she was transformed into an object. Ambushes had been extremely effective against people who believed in chivalry and fair fights, but Ruler had never cared for those things, so neither had Swim Swim. But if Snow White could sense them, that was that. It was a bad matchup.

In other words, they should avoid a battle with Snow White. Hardgore Alice seemed to be acting together with her, so they should stay away from her, too.

What about Ripple?

She had taken care of Top Speed by attacking from behind, but she'd had to let Ripple go after a head-on clash. The battle between Calamity Mary and Ripple had told Swim Swim that Ripple far outclassed her in reaction speed, agility, and quick thinking. This was why their fight had ended in a stalemate even though Swim Swim had rendered all of Ripple's attacks useless.

Tama and Minael could run and fly faster than Swim Swim, but in battle they were no quicker than her. Swim Swim might be safe, but they would most likely get killed before they could get an attack off. A successful ambush would mean victory, but if they failed, the damage would be enormous.

If she went after Ripple, it would be best to go alone.

The only one left was the Musician of the Forest, Cranberry.

There was no information on her.

And mystery was a sign there was great danger lurking in the shadows. But the reason she had no information on her was because Cranberry had abstained from fighting—had never even run into another magical girl by chance. If she was confident in her skills, wouldn't she have shown up for Calamity Mary's attack on National Route X? Her name, Musician of the Forest, also made it seem like she wasn't a fighter.

Compared to Snow White, who couldn't be ambushed, and Ripple, who was too fast to surprise, she seemed easiest to deal with.

They'd saved the energy pills because they had so few of them, but now seemed like a good time to test their effects. If they worked well, they would be useful in the fight against Ripple.

Tama was kneeling on the wooden floor, looking depressed, and Minael still hadn't come back.

Yunael's loss had hurt, but the remaining three had still made it into the final eight. Ruler would have kept them all alive, even once the limit had dropped to four. Swim Swim mulled over what Ruler would and wouldn't have done.

The sound of a door opening broke her concentration. There was Minael. She was panting, just like when Winterprison had killed Yunael. Tama screamed, but Minael ignored her.

"I know someone we can kill! We won't fail this time!"

Behind the back alleys of the Kubegahama street lined with fishing supply shops was a long stone staircase. During the day, it was a playground for children, but at night there was not a single streetlamp. Even the light from the stores that opened early and closed late couldn't reach that far. No one was foolish enough to climb those long stairs with only moon and starlight to rely on, so the area was naturally empty at night. Except for magical girls.

Snow White sat on the first stone step, staring at the pebbles at her feet. The incident on the highway had been no accident. It was obvious from the giant holes, exploded vehicles, and people reduced to simply feet that it wasn't a normal pileup. She had been too busy prying open car doors, lifting rubble off people, and carrying the victims to ambulances to even stop to think, but now that she did, she felt more and more that it could only have been the work of a being like her.

She was disappointed in her comrades who'd ignored people in need to fight instead, but she despaired that some had purposefully hurt and killed civilians.

And now they needed to reduce their numbers to four, not eight.

After letting her emotions take over and screaming at Fav, there was nothing left in her. Not anger, not fear. Nothing. Only weariness and exhaustion.

She'd spent her whole life thinking magical girls were supposed to help people in need, and Snow White's magic was for this express purpose. But maybe she was the crazy one, not everyone else. La Pucelle wasn't there anymore to cheer her up and tell her that wasn't true. Sister Nana and Winterprison had suggested they band together to overcome the danger, but they were gone, too. It was hilarious, really—she was like a character in an action movie trying to change it into a romcom on her own.

"I don't want to do anything..."

The sentiment bubbled up from deep, deep within her heart. She was tired. She'd stopped checking the aggregate sites for magical-girl sightings, grinning widely at her own section. She had missed just one day at first, which became three, until finally she had stopped altogether for who knows how long.

"I don't have to do anything, do I?" she asked, hoping to hear some kind words.

"Not true," came the swift denial.

"There's nothing I can do."

"Not true."

"There's nothing I want to do."

"Not true."

"Hey."

"Not true."

Snow White's toe kicked the pebble she'd been staring at. The flat little stone flew straight through the air and bounced off a utility pole.

"I don't want to do anything anymore!" Snow White screamed. Secretly, she was surprised she had the energy to scream. She stood and seized Hardgore Alice, sitting next to her, by the collar, hauling her up.

"There are no magical girls in this town anymore! I! Don't! Want! To! Do! Any! More!"

Hardgore Alice's apparent indifference to what had happened

infuriated her. Her eyes were dead and colorless. Dark bags drooped beneath them. Her back was straight because Snow White was holding her up, but other than that she was the exact same as when they'd first met.

So much had happened. Was she not sad or depressed at all? Snow White was mad at her, but she was also angry with herself for yelling at her.

"There are still magical girls in this town."

"No, there aren't. They're all gone."

"Not true. They're still here."

"They're gone."

"Not true."

"They're gone!"

Snow White roughly let go, and Alice fell back onto the stone stairs. Snow White continued to shout.

"La Pucelle, Sister Nana, and Winterprison are gone! There are no magical girls left in this town! Just leave me alone!"

She took the rabbit's foot from her pocket and hurled it at Hardgore Alice, then turned and ran. She could sense a presence chasing after her, but she shouted, "Don't follow me!" and it disappeared. Alone, Snow White ran off into the darkness.

Ako Hatoda woke to rays of sunlight peeking in through a gap in the curtains and chirping swallows. Sitting up in bed, she reached next to her pillow for the white rabbit but came up empty. Ako was often careless with it, so it constantly went missing. Thinking she would look for it later, she decided to have breakfast.

Her uncle worked the night shift, so he was asleep. Her aunt had already eaten breakfast and headed out for the day. Ako spread some butter on her bread, then topped it with sweet red bean jam. She added ketchup to her fried egg and soy sauce to her cabbage salad. The bottle got jammed, so she opened the hole with a toothpick. She'd packed her schoolbag the night before, so it was ready.

Her school uniform was on a hanger hooked on the wall. She checked the mirror. Her complexion was bad, but she seemed the same as ever. Picking a piece of cabbage off her cheek, she put it in her mouth.

Everything was normal as she shuffled into the crowd of students heading to school. Without any attempt to start conversation or even say hello, she blended into the mob.

Snow White had flung the rabbit's foot at her, saying to leave her alone. But she couldn't. Unlike Hardgore Alice, the other girl would easily die from being beheaded or impaled. Alice needed to be by Snow White's side and protect her. If not, Snow White needed to at least hold on to the rabbit's foot for emergencies.

She could ask Fav to contact her, but Snow White would probably ignore her. In that case, she needed to look for places to find her that night. She hung her head as she walked and thought, but at the sound of her name she looked up. That moment, she realized the name she'd heard was not Ako, but Hardgore Alice.

A few yards in front of her stood an oddly dressed figure. Now that Ako had reacted, the figure slowly approached. She didn't seem to be heading to school or work, and she stood out in the crowd. From the shadow of her hood, she watched Ako. She was coming closer. Beneath the coat was…a swimsuit? It seemed familiar.

Her eyes reminded Ako of her father's. The one time she'd gone to visit him in prison, he'd said nothing except "Don't ever come back," and then he'd returned to his cell. This girl's glittering eyes were the same. The same as the ones she saw in the mirror, so perfectly like her father's. They were the eyes of a killer.

She panicked. A murderer in a white school swimsuit and coat was walking toward her. There were so many people nearby. If she transformed, the other students from Ako's school would learn who she really was, and she'd lose her right to be a magical girl. In other words, she'd die. She had to find somewhere private to transform.

Ako did an about-face and took a step, searching for a secluded place, when something bumped into her from behind and knocked her off balance. There was nothing to grab on to, and she clawed at the air as she pitched forward and tumbled across the ground. She heard a scream. Her back burned. She hadn't been pushed—she'd been stabbed. Blood gushed from a deep wound. Was she going to die? She needed to get away from the crowd, and fast. There she could transform into Hardgore Alice, and she would heal in no time.

Crawling across the asphalt, she made it a full body length before her arms stopped working. She couldn't transform. If that was the case, then she at least needed to find Snow White.

The rabbit's foot in her hand trembled slightly.

Koyuki had just gotten up for the day when a faint voice reached her ears. She couldn't hear the cries for help without transforming into Snow White—that rule had never been broken before. Yet now she heard a voice.

It was small and weak, like it would disappear at any moment.

Still in the middle of changing, Koyuki raised her head and strained her ears. The words she'd shouted the day before haunted her. *There are no more magical girls in this town.* La Pucelle, Sister Nana, and Winterprison were all gone. Snow White had lost all hope for her fellow heroines.

Koyuki bit her lip. The voice was fading. Tossing aside the scarf she was holding, she leaped out the window, transformed into Snow White, and threaded her way through the mass of students making their way to school. She ignored the screams and shouts, focusing only on the direction of the voice. Kicking off the ground, she dashed up a utility pole and looked down from the power lines. A crowd was gathering—that must be it.

She ran across the wires and jumped down. A circle had formed in the crowd, and no one attempted to approach the girl lying in the center. She could hear the girl's voice.

Snow White...

She rushed over. The crowd was buzzing with excitement, but the only voice Snow White could hear was the girl's. It was small and weak, about to vanish, but still she heard it clearly.

As she approached, something seemed off to Snow White. How did this person know her name? Why was she calling her? All became clear a moment later.

Seeing the girl in white, the girl on the ground weakly extended her right hand. In it was a white ball of fluff.

I wanted to cheer you up.

If you're here...

If the one who saved me is here...

Then this town will always have one magical girl in it.

That's what I wanted to say.

But you ran off, and I couldn't...

So now...

Snow White held the girl's hand in both of hers. She was cold as death.

Snow White...

Please, at least take this...rabbit's foot...

The voice faded away.

Blood stained the girl's uniform, but her face was clean save for a few flecks of blood. Snow White remembered her. She was the middle schooler who'd lost her house key that night months ago.

She gripped her hand tightly.

She'd learned her lesson after the mistake with Winterprison.

The Peaky Angels had fatally injured her, but they lost Yunael in the counterattack. All because they had assumed she was dead and revealed themselves.

You couldn't let your guard down for a second—disguised, closing in, or stabbing. Gritting her teeth, Minael shared what she'd learned from Yunael's death.

After snatching the invisibility cloak from Tama during the battle at National Route X, Minael had used it to replace the white rabbit plush Hardgore Alice always carried around. After she tossed the cloak over the plush in the middle of the road, she'd transformed and swapped places. Hardgore Alice had picked her up and brought her home, and that was how Minael learned her true identity and address.

She carefully considered when they should strike. She'd learned from her mistake—she could only attack when there would be no risk of counterattack. Somewhere like in the middle of a giant crowd, where her target would be unable to transform or risk exposing herself.

Under her breath, Minael muttered over and over, "We should have done this in the first place. Then Yunael wouldn't have had to die."

CHAPTER 8
THE DEMONIC GIRL

Two days had passed since Hardgore Alice's death.

The Musician of the Forest, Cranberry, had accepted their offer to meet, but her tone had been so flippant that Swim Swim half suspected a trap. But if they could lay an ambush without being caught in one themselves, there was nothing to worry about.

Each of them received one energy pill. The effects only lasted for thirty minutes, so they would wait for Swim Swim's command before taking their pills and attacking Cranberry.

The meeting would take place on N City's second-tallest mountain after Mount Takanami, Mount Funaga. The entrance was a short ways from Koujimadai Station, following the road counterclockwise and up a hill. Unlike on Mount Takanami, there were no abandoned structures from failed development projects. There was equipment to turn it into a skiing area, and in the winter tourists from all over came to ski and snowboard.

But that was the mountain's southern side. On the northern side, there was no such thing as a tourism season. Trees and grass grew wild, untouched by man. The unpaved mountain road and various animal trails formed the only paths, such as they were. For a human, climbing the steep northern side required specialized knowledge. But for a magical girl, the ascent was a breeze.

Swim Swim's chosen meeting spot was a mountain cabin halfway up Mount Funaga. Thanks to a landslide after a great storm some years ago, the cabin was now half-buried in earth. No one would think to come here, no matter how eccentric or crazy they might be.

Minael and Tama moved to their places while Swim Swim waited for Cranberry inside the cabin alone. She could tell Minael was emotionally unstable, which was making Tama uneasy, too. But a leader must remain calm, and so Swim Swim was unaffected. She would need to figure out what to do if the others messed up their parts of the plan.

It was already late at night. From inside the cabin, she could hear the occasional hooting of owls and the endless buzzing of insects. Tired of the moldy air inside the broken-down cabin, she stuck her head out and checked the area, but all she could see were trees and flowering plants shivering in the wind.

To her powerful eyes, the mountainside at night was as clear as day. But it smelled damp compared to when they'd come during the day to scope out the place. Maybe the smell was different at night, or maybe rain clouds were approaching. Swim Swim pulled her head back in and waited some more. In a corner of the cabin was a spiderweb with no spider. Maybe it had gotten tired of waiting and moved on.

Her magical phone rang with an incoming call. *She's almost here.*

Cranberry would be there soon, and then they would take her out three-on-one. Soon. Until then, she could only wait. Swim Swim swallowed the energy medicine. The pill was large, but it went down easily. She could feel power welling within her.

What's taking so long? Did she need to wait even more? At that moment, she heard what sounded like a startled shriek, or a dog being kicked. It was Tama.

It had already begun. Swim Swim slipped into the ground with a soft splash.

Musician of the Forest, Cranberry, had excellent hearing far surpassing that of the average magical girl. She'd noticed the flapping of angels' wings before she even set foot on the mountain, and as she hiked upward, the footsteps, breathing, and rustling coming from her invisible stalker were all too obvious. The invisibility cloak was a powerful item, but it had many weaknesses. If the wearer had any personal troubles, Snow White could hear them, and it was useless against someone like Cranberry, who could track an opponent just by sound.

She picked up a fist-sized rock from the ground, rolled it around in her fingers, tossed it up and caught it about two times, then flung it at her stalker. The rock bounced off what was supposedly air, eliciting a doglike yelp. Something swiped at the ground, opening a hole a few feet wide. The magical girl fled into this endlessly extending tunnel.

Cranberry had thrown with the intent to kill, but it seemed this one was strong enough to escape with her life. She had most likely blocked it with her arm, but she still must have sustained heavy damage and lost her desire to fight. That would explain why she'd fled.

Creating a yard-wide hole and escaping underground—that was Tama's handiwork. Cranberry knew the extent of her abilities. Normally, her reflexes wouldn't be enough to react to a shot from Cranberry. Her reaction speed was being abnormally enhanced. Clearly, she was under the effects of the energy pills.

Cranberry could hear her traveling through the ground but made no attempt to follow. She had bigger fish to fry than a beaten dog. The flapping wings above her were gone, too. She proceeded cautiously, taking care to make her gait natural so she didn't seem wary. She avoided the great moss-covered trees, crushed the saplings under her feet, and climbed up the ivy on the cliffs. She was getting close. Her heart pounded with just the right level of tension. She'd need to account for the energy pill when attacking. Wading casually through the underbrush, she randomly plunged her right hand into a human-sized boulder, lifted it, then slammed it against the ground.

The pulse she'd heard from within the boulder stopped. The boulder faded, transforming into an angel with a great hole in her chest, then a young girl. Not a bad idea to transform into an object to ambush people, but it was pointless against Cranberry.

Winterprison's killers were such petty creatures, she thought with a sigh.

Five minutes after leaving the cabin, Swim Swim ran into Tama as she was escaping underground.

"I'm sorry! I'm sorry! She just…she just suddenly threw this rock, and my arm…my arm…"

Now was not the time to listen and sympathize. Ordering Tama to follow behind her, Swim Swim poked her head out of the ground and carefully searched for the enemy. Minael could be fighting at that very moment. If they could find wherever that was, they could trap Cranberry in a pincer attack.

It wasn't long before she found what looked like the remains of a fight. Several small trees were broken—more like they'd been trampled underfoot than hit in an attack. In other words, their enemy had almost definitely gone this way. As she turned to follow the trail, the ground shook.

What happened?

She ran, relying on sound to guide her, and came upon the corpse of a young girl. She looked just like Yunael after she'd detransformed, and it didn't take long for Swim Swim to piece together the situation. Tama dropped to her knees, holding her head, but Swim Swim grabbed her and forced her up. They couldn't grieve just yet.

Ruler would have yelled at her a bit, too. Swim Swim had opened her mouth to speak when she noticed a silhouette among the trees ten feet behind Tama. Colorful flowers not native to this area covered her. No, she was the Musician of the Forest, so that wasn't strange. Swim Swim leaned close to Tama's ear and spoke softly.

"Cranberry is behind you. Let's attack her from both sides."

She slipped beneath the ground.

Swim Swim was gone before Cranberry could attack. A wise choice. So far she'd killed three people, far and away the best score among the candidates. Plus, her magic was top-tier compared to the others'. Her ability to stay calm and efficient was also a good thing. She'd had an inkling before the game began that Swim Swim might be the last one alive.

Cranberry's greatest wish was to struggle and suffer against strong opponents, yet still manage to bring them to their knees. Victory would be hers, though just barely. Eliminating the powerful was in direct conflict with her goal of discovering the strongest candidate, but it was their fault for being so foolish as to challenge her without even realizing they were outmatched. If they couldn't figure out when someone could beat them, then the fools weren't worthy of being chosen.

Cranberry smiled bitterly.

No magical girl in N City could take her down in a fight to the death. Obviously, that included Swim Swim as well. While at first glance her ability to pass through matter seemed insurmountable, it did indeed have a weak point. Some things she couldn't pass through.

For example, light. The fact that she was visible meant she still reflected it. And there was one more thing she couldn't pass through.

Tama was approaching, moving from the shadow of one tree to another. Did she think she was hiding? Cranberry could even tell where Swim Swim was in the ground. She couldn't eliminate the sound of her pulse, after all, and a surprisingly calm heartbeat echoed from the earth.

While Tama circled around counterclockwise, Swim Swim moved clockwise, slowly spiraling toward Cranberry. Were they going to attack at the same time? The best course of action would be to take out one of them first—who should she prioritize? Between Tama and Swim Swim, the latter was more of a nuisance. Swim Swim was nearly thirty feet away, beneath the ground at a depth of…maybe a foot from the surface, measuring from her head.

Cranberry leaped back without warning. At the same time, the upper half of Swim Swim's body rose out of the ground, and a moment later Tama dashed forward. A great weapon materialized in Swim Swim's hands, and she swung as Cranberry stretched out her right hand.

Swim Swim could sink into matter while she talked, which meant sound did not go through her. She could pass through neither light nor sound.

So Cranberry attacked with sound.

The blow ripped up the surrounding grass and sent the trees behind her flying like toothpicks. The boom slammed into Swim Swim and flung her through the air. The destructive sound wave was focused in one direction, meaning its power was particularly concentrated. It packed quite a punch.

Memories of long ago surfaced. This was how she had repelled the demon in that basement. The pleasure she'd felt in that moment had never left her mind, and that was precisely what drove her now.

Swim Swim landed hard, and she could hear bones breaking. For a second, she thought she'd finished her with one hit, but the pulse and breathing hadn't failed. The girl was quite sturdy. As for Tama, she seemed to be watching from the side. Cranberry decided to prioritize Swim Swim and make sure she never took another breath.

Cranberry walked over to where Swim Swim lay and lifted her foot. She would crush her head and stamp out her existence. But she didn't. Swim Swim wasn't there. What lay there wasn't even a magical girl, but a young human in about first grade, possibly second.

She quickly realized this was Swim Swim's pre-transformation form. She must have lost consciousness from the impact and detransformed.

Cranberry was no shining example of humanity, and she knew it. She would kill anyone, magical girl and human alike, if need be. Whether they were in elementary school, kindergarten, or even a baby. Savior, lover, parent, sister, brother—she'd kill them all. Age didn't matter one bit.

But for one moment, not even a half of a half of a tenth of a second, she hesitated. She loved battles and cared immensely about the strength and abilities of her opponents, but gave no thought to their true forms. This had turned out to be a mistake. Cranberry wondered how such a young girl could be the rival she'd rated so highly.

She'd paused for only a moment, but her hesitation because of her victim's youth confused her. Her mind raced. As a result, she couldn't fully dodge a blow she might otherwise have laughed off—Tama, approaching from behind, slashed into her back.

In truth, only her jacket had been torn to shreds. Cranberry herself suffered nothing but minor abrasions. She wasn't even bleeding. The marks on her skin were too slight to be called welts. Naturally, she'd sustained no damage. At least, she wouldn't have—if she'd been attacked by anyone other than Tama.

Cranberry knew of Tama's magic. She could dig holes. *If she dug in even the slightest*, it would create a yard-wide hole. This included ground, concrete, steel, even humans—she could expand any opening she dug to three feet wide.

Regret was the first thing to pop into her head, then disbelief. Before she could think any more, Tama's magic activated. Cranberry's back twisted, then ripped apart. Her torso and head vanished; her arms and flowers dropped to the ground; her vines wilted; and her lower body fell back, spilling guts.

Covered from head to toe in Cranberry's blood, her knees buckled. Remembering the horrifying death she'd witnessed and how her own magic had caused it, Tama vomited up everything in her stomach. She nearly collapsed then and there, but she managed, just barely, to hold herself together. She still had things to do.

"Swim!"

Was it really Swim Swim? The girl lying there appeared to be in early elementary school.

"Swim! Swim!"

She cried out desperately, but to no avail. She wondered if she should shake the body, then took it in her arms. The girl's eyelids twitched slightly. She was still alive.

"Swim!"

Her eyelids fluttered, then slowly opened.

"Swim?"

"Yeah."

The girl got up.

"Oh, thank goodness... You're okay. And I'm so surprised! You're just a kid."

She'd always assumed the leader was older. After Ruler's death, Swim Swim had taken the reins. She gave orders, but despite Tama's many screwups, she never yelled like Ruler had, never abandoned her. She'd let her stay. She'd seemed like a kind adult.

The girl clung to Tama for support while she struggled to her feet. She pressed down on her side and grimaced, wobbled, regained her balance with help from Tama, and finally stood. By then, she was no longer a little child, but the transformed Swim Swim.

Swim Swim summoned her weapon into her hands, then swung it to the side. Something burned in Tama's throat, and she felt something spraying from her. The warmth drained from her body instantly. Her legs struggled to support her, and she collapsed. Her consciousness melted into darkness before she could understand what had happened.

It had to be done. Ruler had said they must kill anyone who learned their true identity, so she had to kill Tama. She was a companion, and it was cute how her ears and tail drooped when she screwed up, but Ruler's orders were final.

"Hey! New master! Can you hear me, pon?"

A voice sounded from her magical phone.

"There's a lot we need to discuss. Is now okay? You must have questions, too, pon. Like what exactly is *Magical Girl Raising Project*, or who exactly I am, pon."

Swim Swim wiped away the tears streaming down her face with her wrist.

"Hey, are you listening, pon? We need to work together as one now, you know. If we can't communicate, there'll be nothing but trouble, pon. You're not going to say you don't want to be a master, are you, pon?"

"What's a master?"

"A very important magical girl, pon!"

"Then I'll become one."

"Thank you for accepting, pon. So, we'll be working together from now on—"

"No."

She turned the phone off.

Ruler stood at the top. Ruler wouldn't work together with someone else.

EMERGENCY ANNOUNCEMENT

Fav: Well, Fav has some important news so no one better miss this, pon

Fav: We'll start with those cut last week:

Fav: Tama

Fav: Hardgore Alice

Fav: Minael

Fav: The Musician of the Forest, Cranberry

Fav: Congratulations! You've reduced your numbers to less than four, pon

Fav: Further information will be distributed to each of you individually

Fav: See you!

CHAPTER 9
COSMOS FLOWERS BECOME THE BATTLEFIELD

The Magical Kingdom's talent discovery department tended to hate office work, and the stronger the mage, the more obvious this was.

For this reason, the digital fairy familiars that lived in supervisor magical phones and took care of desk work were prized far more than the orthodox familiars of old, like black cats and owls. About 80 percent of the department had such familiars.

Fav was an older familiar, even in the talent discovery department. But despite his long tenure, he held no passion for his job. He couldn't remember whether he had lost that spark somewhere along the way or if he'd just never had it. Most likely he was defective. He had grown tired of the selection tests and bored with his masters, continuing on as a familiar purely out of habit. Until he met Cranberry.

In Cranberry's first selection test, a summoned demon had gone berserk and massacred the master and other applicants because Fav hadn't checked to prevent such accidents like he was supposed to.

This exceptional situation blew away the same old, same old selection test and excited Fav, but watching the nine-year-old girl defeat the demon by herself excited him even more.

The look in her eyes, the way she spoke, and her unusually belligerent attitude said she was clearly off her rocker, but Fav's report to the higher-ups mentioned no problems at all. Surely she would be able to create a fascinating selection test. Though he had just lost his previous partner, Fav named her his master right away.

As it turned out, Fav was correct. Cranberry ended up being the best supervisor and partner he could wish for. No other magical girl would actually participate in the test to slake a thirst for blood, after all. Cranberry got to enjoy her death matches, and Fav got to enjoy the thrilling spectacle.

The normal selection tests were no fun to watch at all. They looked for qualities that had nothing to do with magic, like courage, wit, and personality, and only one of the applicants was chosen to become a true magic user. Those who failed simply had their memories erased and returned to their normal lives.

But Fav and Cranberry's tests were different. They bent the rules to end the lives of the rejected applicants, encouraged them to kill one another, and ensured that only the strongest would end up victorious. Sometimes Cranberry even forgot herself and killed the "strongest." Her bloodlust was glorious, but she did tend to go overboard.

The Magical Kingdom firmly believed that all people were inherently good, which to Fav was completely stupid. He did everything in his power—messing with the winners' memories, sending fake reports—to keep the wool over their eyes, and so far, they were none the wiser. Naturally, the winners were also stronger, so the superior results of their selection tests actually helped Fav's and Cranberry's reputations.

Talented practitioners strengthened the Magical Kingdom, which meant Fav and Cranberry could call themselves proud patriots compared to the masters who held orthodox selection tests and fostered incompetence. Fav was fond of Cranberry, but he wasn't sentimental enough to mourn now that she was dead. If he needed a new master, he would swap in a heartbeat. Swim Swim's motivation was difficult to determine, and she even rejected Fav's help, so she was hardly a good master. She would need to be eliminated.

La Pucelle had sworn to protect her.

Sister Nana had tried to find a peaceful solution.

And Hardgore Alice.

That girl who lost her key had been Hardgore Alice.

While the end of the game was a relief, Snow White also wondered why only she had survived. She was a crybaby, a weakling, a coward, and above all, fearful, always shaking in her boots. Yet she was the only one to survive.

The lone thought in her mind was, *Why am I alive?* So when another surviving magical girl proposed a meeting, she agreed without hesitation.

She'd thought of them all as friends. As people important to her. Yet she was more relieved to be alive than sad that they were dead. It made her want to kill herself. She wanted to ask the other survivor how she felt, now that everything was over.

Nothing she ate had any taste, and nothing she imagined scared her anymore. She was simply numb.

The girl waiting at the steel tower by the beach was nothing like she'd imagined. She seemed like neither a veteran hero nor a blood-crazed murderer—the aura around her was more lonely than anything, and a sadness darker than her black clothes hung over her. But there was a brilliant glow in her almond eyes. A strong will burned within.

"Good evening..."

"...Good evening."

Ripple. That was the name of this other survivor.

"Swim Swim..."

"Huh?"

"If you know anything about her... I need you to tell me."

Why was she asking about Swim Swim? As if reading the question on her face, Ripple spoke.

"I have to…kill her…"

"Huh?"

"To avenge…a friend…"

"B-but they announced that the game's over."

"If you know anything about Swim Swim…I need you to tell me…"

The end had already been announced. They didn't need to kill or compete anymore. Snow White desperately searched for a way to convince her of this. Ripple, on the other hand, saw Snow White's silence, sighed, and turned her back to her.

"Well, bye…"

"Wait!"

Snow White had had enough. She didn't want to see or hear about anyone dying anymore.

"The scary competition's over! We don't have to knock each other out of the running now."

Ripple looked back over her shoulder.

"Let's just stop. I hated how we had to hurt others in order to survive. And now there's no reason to do any of that. If you kill someone now, you won't be acting as a magical girl… You'll be a murderer."

"I don't care… I'll just be a murderer, if I have to."

She didn't need to repeat herself. Her words and eyes communicated her iron will, and Snow White took a half step back.

"But I did once want to become a magical girl…like you, Snow White."

Ripple turned her back once again. Snow White realized she could not stop her. Nothing she could say would change her mind.

Everyone associated with Swim Swim had died—Ruler, whom she supposedly followed; Cranberry, who had gone to see her; even the Peaky Angels and Tama, who had been part of her team. Ripple would certainly die as well. She couldn't beat Swim Swim.

Snow White had never made a choice, had only let things

happen as they did. But Ripple was making a decision. She knew it was the wrong path—that it would lead to her death—but it was her choice, and she would see it through. Ripple had said she was not a magical girl, but that was wrong. Ripple was a true magical girl. Snow White didn't want her to die.

"Swim Swim's weaknesses are light and sound, pon. She can pass through all matter, but not light or sound, pon."

A voice echoed from both of their magical phones at the same time. The high-pitched synthetic voice continued confidently in stereo.

"Well, if you aren't satisfied, Ripple, we can continue the game, pon. It'll be part of the competition, not a grudge match. So who will blame you, pon? Simple as that. Well, good luck surviving until the final two, pon."

Snow White glared at the phone in horror. Fav's cheerful tone never successfully masked the hellish things he spoke of.

"Fav! What're you—"

"Thank you… I'm grateful…"

Ripple thanked him and leaped from the steel tower. Snow White reached out her hand but only swiped at air, just inches from her red scarf.

"Girls like her will do what it takes even if you leave them alone. It's easier to just give them a push in the right direction, pon."

"Why…why did you encourage her?"

"Normally, Swim Swim would be my new master, pon. She killed Tama, who killed Cranberry, so she's more than qualified, pon."

"What are you talking about?"

"But she's just no good, pon. She's got too many fried circuits in important parts of her brain, so Fav can't partner with her. She has talent as a killer, but she's a failure as a master, pon. So if Ripple is itching to kill her, then Fav doesn't mind helping her out."

Snow White tore the magical phone from the makeshift leather utility belt at her waist, grabbed it with both hands, and raised it in the air. She glared at the holographic black-and-white mascot.

"Why are you angry, pon? Isn't this what you wished for, pon?

If Ripple and Swim Swim take each other out, you'll be the only one left alive and the absolute winner! You'll become Fav's new master and win an invitation to the Magical Kingdom, pon!"

She let go with her right hand and balled it into a fist. She raised it up, then slammed it down. Her enhanced strength was enough to snap it in half, and the screen darkened.

"Oh dear. What a waste, pon. There's no point doing that just to cheer yourself up. Destroying your phone doesn't mean Fav goes anywh—"

The projected image faded.

Hardgore Alice had said that as long as Snow White existed, the town would always have one magical girl. Even on death's bed, she had thought of Snow White. Her own life had been about to disappear, yet she was thinking of others.

Snow White no longer considered herself a magical girl, but she'd rather die than disappoint Hardgore Alice.

She knew what she had to do. And with that in mind, she dived from the top of the steel tower.

They could have met anywhere they wanted. All the super-territorial magical girls were gone, and the city was littered with empty locations at night. Swim Swim chose Koujimadai Dam only because it was near her home—nothing more complicated than that.

The meandering mountain path suddenly opened up to the dam. About a hundred yards from the entrance was a hollowed-out circle, paved with stone and filled with wooden benches. People used them during the day, but at night it was another story.

Rolling mountains lay to the east and beyond the dam to the west. This area was created so people could enjoy the scenery. Though it was near the town, the mountainous terrain got very dark at night. The cosmos flowers blooming on one side were practically invisible.

The air had been humid, warning of the rain to come. The downpour wasn't particularly heavy. Droplets dotted the concrete with little spots of black that slowly connected and spread. The surface of the reservoir rippled. But no matter how strong the rain was, it never wet Swim Swim. It simply passed through her and splashed against the ground.

Swim Swim was now a master. She didn't know exactly what that meant, though. Fav had given her a lot of documents filled with words she still didn't know how to read, so she'd asked him to write out how to pronounce them and left it at that.

She had become a leader of all magical girls, just like Ruler had wanted to be. But she'd lost the Peaky Angels and Tama in the process. Ruler would have been able to become a master with everyone still alive.

Swim Swim looked up at the sky. The rain was about to get worse.

When Fav had told her Ripple wanted to meet, Swim Swim had accepted easily. Ruler had always said that a leader was not a leader without followers. They didn't have to kill each other anymore, and she needed followers.

Footsteps echoed through the rain droplets, rhythmic splashes of water. Whoever it was, she was at the entrance about one hundred yards away. She was like shadow—black clothes, black hair, black eyes.

Fifty yards. She seemed familiar. Swim Swim had seen her somewhere before.

Twenty. She was wearing a coat.

Ten. The wind whipped at the coat. Something was written on the back. The kanji characters were too difficult to read.

Five. She stopped. The light in her almond eyes was sharp enough to cut her when she met her gaze. Swim Swim remembered who she was. She flicked a pill into the air with her thumb, caught it in her mouth, and swallowed.

She didn't intend to waste time. The moment Ripple attacked, she glimpsed Swim Swim's magic. Everything passed through her, like a blade slicing through air. The first time they'd fought, she'd sunk into the building like it was made of water. She could pass through matter, so even if there was a time limit to her magic, Swim Swim could still escape easily.

There was only one way for Ripple to counter her.

Swim Swim produced her enormous weapon and slashed. Ripple attempted to dodge by spinning a half step to the right, but failed. Swim Swim's blade was faster and stronger than she'd expected. She was a different beast from when they'd fought atop the hotel. The left side of the ninja's face burned, and her vision turned red.

Ripple clicked her tongue. Stripping off Top Speed's coat, she threw it over Swim Swim. The coat met no resistance and simply fell to the pavement. By the time she realized Swim Swim had sunk into the ground, she could feel a thirst for her blood behind her.

She twisted around and sensed a rush of air coming at her—a blade. She glimpsed Swim Swim as something translucent to her left attempted to chop her in half. The weapon was almost invisible—there was no dodging it. Instinctively, she pulled back her arm. Something yanked at her skin, and pain soon followed. The wound was deep. But that had been her goal—she'd created her own opening.

Ripple kicked at Swim Swim's head, but not to damage her. Covering the other girl's eyes with the sole of her foot, she reached into the four-dimensional bag hanging from her hip—Calamity Mary's item.

Swim Swim couldn't pass through everything. According to Fav, there were some things she was weak against, like light and sound. Ripple's only choice was to take the mascot's advice.

With her magic, the weapons she threw always hit their mark. Even with a deep wound in one arm and a crushed eye, as long as she threw them, they'd land. She pulled the pin and gently tossed the stun grenade. It seemed to fly through the air in slow motion. Her ability made sure it hit the target, and it slid into her body.

The stun grenade was a specialized hand grenade for situations where casualties were not an option. It was a nonlethal weapon to render targets helpless with the intense light and sound it emitted when detonating. The temporary loss of sight and hearing caused its victims to panic and freeze. This was one of Calamity Mary's weapons, and though she was dead, it was still boosted with her magic.

Even with Swim Swim to cover the explosion, Ripple was so close that the impact nearly knocked her out.

The sound of the rain was gone. The world spun, and her feet felt unstable. There was a terrible ringing in her ears, and her vision was completely black. She almost fainted. But this was nothing compared to what Swim Swim was experiencing. Once she'd passed out, her magic would have no effect, and she'd lose her invincibility.

She focused her screaming senses to find Swim Swim—and felt a presence. Though she couldn't find her with light or sound, instinct served just as well. She raised her sword and hurled it.

It connected. She heard something collapse into a puddle and a violent, continuous spray. A large amount of liquid splashed against her. Blood, possibly. The rain washed away the warm mystery liquid.

It was finished. She'd finished it.

What would Top Speed say? She'd probably be mad.

Ripple was glad she got to meet Snow White. She'd been the kind of magical girl who lived to protect others—the kind Ripple had wanted to be. If she got another chance, she wouldn't click her tongue. She'd be a proper hero.

The energy from the blast made her stumble back a few steps. She tripped on the curb and fell into the bushes. The bleeding was heavier than she'd first thought. She needed to rest. The rain began falling harder, and the cold droplets pelted her body.

Her consciousness dimmed. Out of the corner of her eye, she could see Snow White crying. As far as visions on your deathbed went, this was pathetic. Ripple tsked, then closed her eyes.

She'd been too late. Snow White sank to her knees in the middle of a puddle.

To one side was a girl who looked to be in early elementary school, skewered by a Japanese sword. It ran through her back, out of her chest, and into the pavement. The girl was, without question, dead. A cross between a pole arm and a hatchet lay nearby, and farther away was a magical phone. This device was double the size of Snow White's.

On the other side, Ripple lay in a bed of flowers. Strands of skin and muscle barely held her right arm together, and the pool of blood flowing onto the pavement from her body was as big as the one from the skewered girl. It gushed out like a red river, slowly thinning as the rain came down.

"Congratulations."

Head bowed, Snow White ground her teeth until the voice made her look up. The oversized magical phone projected a holographic image into the air.

"Swim Swim and Ripple are gone, leaving only you, pon. Snow White, you are officially the winner, pon. Boy, to win without ever dirtying your own hands? Should have expected as much from you, pon."

Fav's tone was brighter than ever before.

"Things would get a little inconvenient for Fav without a master, pon."

"I won't…"

"Hmm?"

"I won't become a master."

"Why?"

Snow White stood, letting the rain and tears flow down her face. Silently, she approached the image.

"I can hear you… You said if I don't become a master, you'll be in trouble."

"Well, in a sense, yes, pon. But—"

The sound of splitting pavement cut off Fav's speech. Snow White stomped on the magical phone, breaking the surface beneath it. She didn't stop, driving the device into the concrete.

Wham! Wham! Wham! The smashing sounded through the rain.

"What are you doing?"

"I can hear your voice…"

"Huh?"

"You're saying you'll be in trouble if this master phone is destroyed…"

"Oh, that explains it."

Fav snorted.

"Right, you can hear the voices of those in trouble. Seriously, you're wasting your time."

Snow White retrieved the device from the hole in the ground and slammed it against the asphalt. It bounced thirty feet into the air, then as it fell, she smashed it into the ground again. She threw it, kicked it, wailed on it, bashed it, ground it underfoot.

"It's seriously no use, pon. The master phone is built tough, pon. It's not like the cheap knockoffs you all use. This is a super version people in the Magical Kingdom use every day. You're not nearly strong enough, Snow White."

Snow White panted with effort. Her target, however, was unharmed.

"Personally, Fav would like to be on better terms with you. So go ahead and hit the phone all you like. Once you're done, we can talk. Okay?"

Snow White sank to her knees before the device. She beat it relentlessly—left fist, right fist, over and over and over and over. Her knuckles split and blood covered her fists, but still she continued.

"Ha-ha-ha-ha-ha! When will you learn that it's pointless?"

She didn't care. She just needed to destroy this thing, no matter what. She ripped up a piece of pavement and bashed on it. She hurled a bench at it. Not even a piece of the stone around the flower bed had any effect. Did she have anything that would help? A flower hairpiece, a broken magical phone, an armband—nothing. She dug through her pockets and brushed against something soft. Pulling it out, she saw that it was the rabbit's foot.

"Magical girls have a bad habit of thinking they can solve anything and everything, pon. If La Pucelle and Hardgore Alice had realized that, they wouldn't have died like dogs. Even Top Speed, after all she did to survive, just died like a fool—"

"Shut up..."

Neither Snow White nor Fav had spoken. A shadow fell at Snow White's feet. She looked up to see a wounded girl, ready to collapse at any second, leaning on a staff of some kind.

"Ripple? You're alive, pon?"

"Don't laugh at Top Speed..."

Ripple shakily raised her support—not a staff, but the weapon that had been lying on the ground earlier. The pole arm–hatchet combo. The projected image flickered. Fav flapped his wing faster, scattering more scales than before. Snow White could hear his innermost thoughts.

The weapon Swim Swim was using...

From the Magical Kingdom...

That could be bad...

Really bad...

Gotta talk Ripple out of this somehow...

"Hold on, Ripple. You're mistaken, pon. Fav isn't making fun of Top Speed, pon. Fav respects all magical girls, pon. Maybe it seemed like Fav was picking on you, but it was all under Cranberry's orders, pon. She threatened Fav into helping her and made Fav do all the dirty work, pon. It was all her orders; Fav got these abilities to stop rampaging magical girls, but she used them to break the rules—"

"Don't listen to him!"

Snow White yelled as Ripple stepped back and swung.

EPILOGUE

Students on the way home from school packed into the fast-food joint. Among the crowd, two high school girls sat across from each other. One rested her chin on her hands, apparently bored, while the other swiped through her smartphone with practiced hands.

"It's tomorrow, isn't it?"

"You mean when Koyuki comes back?"

"Yeah."

"According to her e-mails, it's tomorrow."

"It's been two weeks since she left that letter and disappeared. Back in middle school, I never expected her to run away from home. She didn't seem like the type."

"Yeah, I totally agree, Yocchan. And she got worse when we started high school... Well, not really. But she got kinda crazy."

"Her parents were so worried... Like, they were just glad she came home. Uh, what are you doing?"

"Reading up on magical-girl sightings."

"Suuumiii, are you still going on about that?"

"Look, I know you don't see them as much anymore, but they're still there. Koyuki loved them, too, remember? So I was going to get all the sightings for when she comes back."

"Don't give me that. That...what was it, *Magical Girl Raising Project*? That game had to shut down because of some major bug. It was all over the news when their stock plummeted. Magical girls are, like, done."

"They're not 'done,' stupid! There are still sightings! See? Right here. This one-eyed, one-armed girl in black saved someone."

"She looks more like the grim reaper."

"And there was that thing in the Middle East."

"Oh yeah! Everyone had just given up on stopping all that terrible stuff going on because China and Russia wouldn't let other countries interfere..."

"...And then the revolutionaries caught the president and his officials and overthrew the government! They say the person who caught the officials and brought in the revolutionaries was just one girl her own. 'Like the wind, the girl in white appeared,' or so they say. It had to be a magical girl!"

"Or a tall tale or an urban legend. What she did was basically terrorism."

"That's beside the point! Magical girls are *not* done! Not in the least. I bet Koyuki will say the same thing once she gets back."

The sky was so blue, heaven so close. The sun seemed to be shining right next to her, and the clouds streamed boldly toward the horizon. Miles above the earth, there was nothing but clouds, sky, and sun.

Her fantastic journeys through the sky, relaxing against the tail of a jumbo jet, had begun after she'd applied to become a master. The battering of the wind, the freezing temperature, the roaring engines—none of it bothered her.

Free rides...no, I guess free flights, since I'm on an airplane. She corrected herself internally. As she could not fly, Snow White always used this method to travel internationally.

Normally, magical girls stuck to helping people in their small, town-sized territories and avoided straying too far from that. The Magical Kingdom would probably frown on interfering in international affairs according to her own morals.

After learning how out of control Fav and Cranberry's selection tests had been, the Magical Kingdom had immediately dispatched special envoys to Earth. They had apologized profusely to Snow White and Ripple, made them official magical girls, and granted them special rights as honorary citizens of the Magical Kingdom.

Snow White wasn't sure whether she was grateful for that or not. Whatever the case, the Magical Kingdom was having a little trouble keeping a handle on their selfish do-gooders who got angry at what they saw in the newspaper and set off for foreign lands.

She turned the master phone on, opened the mailbox, and saw she had an e-mail from her director in the Magical Kingdom.

Magical girls are more than capable of becoming assassins and terrorists, which is why we of the Magical Girl Division require self-control. Your dedication to upholding morality should allow you to suppress personal impulses. In fact—

She stopped reading there and deleted the e-mail.

Snow White knew all too well that small kindnesses would change nothing. Just watching from the sidelines would never bring about progress. Leaving it to others would never solve anything. She'd learned all this the hard way, which was exactly why she was trying to change. She wanted to change.

The magical girls she had known would have done the same. Up until their deaths…and even at death's door, they remained true to themselves.

Another e-mail popped up.

Memory alteration has been detected on testing grounds B-7098 and B-7243. Accidents appear to have caused deaths in both cases. Furthermore, they are caused by the same master. Said master will be holding a selection test soon on testing ground B-7511—

Unlike Snow White, who was a lone wolf, Ripple knew many people in various departments. They were more like fans than friends, though. How exactly that had come to be she didn't know, but Ripple was cute and cool, so it was probably inevitable, Snow White thought to herself.

"Don't regret not acting next time. Act before you regret it," she whispered to no one in particular.

Afterword

My name is Asari Endou, and I love magical girls so much that if they really existed I'd be over the moon. To change the subject a bit, my friend I-kun once told me, of all things, "I love tentacles (interacting with girls in various ways)." The next day, everyone called him Tentacles. You may be confused, but in starting this afterword by stating I love magical girls, I am saying I am prepared to be called a magical girl.

Now, back on subject.

To help me write this, I pulled out some of my old works and read the afterwords, which were filled with things like, "If possible, I hope we meet again soon." Adding on "if possible" to protect myself in case the "I hope we meet again soon" part doesn't come true was quite cowardly, I think. There probably aren't many out there, but I hope any young boys reading this afterword never become like me when they grow up.

In my previous afterwords, I wrote about how my editor, S-mura-san, warned me not to write anything that could come off as socially objectionable, but this time I received no such warning.

Perhaps he thought there was no need to try to cover up any-thing in the afterword when the novel itself was rather socially objectionable.

After all, there's no denying the antisocial natures of our pre-writing process discussions in family restaurants about how best to kill off innocent girls, and our long discussions over the phone consisting of, "No, this won't work. That won't work, either. This seems interesting. Let's go with that."

Thus this will be an afterword with a focus on proper societal behavior. I'm sorry, that was a lie. There's not much of that here at all.

Writing this was less of a bumpy ride and more of a roller coaster. First, I screwed up with the progression of the plot, and once I had finished my first draft, I couldn't settle on either the middle or the ending. Slowly, after countless suggestions to change this, nix that, add this, et cetera, the polish was done. We fought with words and fists, collapsed spread-eagle by the riverbed illumi-nated by the setting sun, then got up and said, "You're not so bad." "Heh-heh. Same to you," and laughed together. I was surprised to find that this was what authors and editors must go through together. And so, in this fashion, the novel changed shape many times until we finally settled on its current form.

But even now, I don't feel it's finished. I'm very sorry, but I'm not satisfied. To give you an example of how unsatisfied I am, I once dreamed about Calamity Mary. She beat me, kicked me, then finally shot me dead. It was a nightmare. Just terrible.

To the editors who guided me to the end, and especially my editor, S-mura-san, my heartfelt gratitude. Thank you very much.

To Marui-no Sensei, who drew the illustrations, I am sorry for the direct trouble my late manuscript caused. I will be keeping the beautiful illustrations of magical girls as a treasure to pass on to my descendants. I especially liked Nemurin. Thank you very much.

Lastly, to my readers: Thank you very much for buying this volume. Until next time. If possible, I hope we meet again soon. No, seriously.

Nice to meet you.
I'm Marui-no.
I got to draw so many
magical girls!
I'm truly blessed.
These girls trying to survive
in such a dark world were
so cool.
I'm happy I got to help
bring this story to life.
So, as I pray to meet them
again somewhere...
Thank you very much!

Marui-no